The Widows

The Widows

Suzette Mayr

NeWest Press · Edmonton

CANADIAN CATALOGUING IN PUBLICATION DATA

Mayr, Suzette.
 The widows

 ISBN 1-896300-30-8

 I. Title.
PS8576.A9W52 1998   C813'.54   C98-910207-6
PR9199.3.M422W52 1998

Editor for the Press: Aritha van Herk
Cover design: Brenda Burgess
Text design: Val Speidel

NeWest Press gratefully acknowledges the support of the Canada Council for the Arts for our publishing program and The Alberta Foundation for the Arts, a beneficiary of the Lottery Fund of the Government of Alberta.

Thank you to the Local History Department, Niagara Falls, New York, Public Library for permission to use the photo of Annie Edson Taylor on the cover.

Excerpts from Pierre Burton's *Niagara: A History of the Falls* copyright 1992 by Pierre Berton Enterprises Limited and published in 1992 by McClelland & Stewart, Inc., reprinted with the kind permission of the author.

Excerpts from Gordon Donaldson's *Niagara!: The Eternal Circus*, copyright 1979 by Gordon Donaldson and published in 1979 by Doubleday Canada Ltd., reprinted with the kind permission of the author.

Every effort has been made to obtain permission for quoted material. If there is an omission or error the author and publisher would be grateful to be so informed.

Printed and bound in Canada

NeWest Publishers Limited
Suite 201, 8540 - 109 Street
Edmonton, Alberta T6G 1E6

For Luise Mayr, Dorle Riedl,
Elisabeth Krischker & Nicole Markotić

Acknowledgements

I am grateful to Aritha van Herk, Nicole Markotic, and Rosemary Nixon for their editorial expertise and support. I would also like to thank Rose-Marie Mayr, Ulrich Mayr, and Margarete Markotic for their help in the areas of geriatrics and German culture. And for the important miscellaneous, a great big thank you to Renée Lang, Lisa Brawn, Denise Groulx, Donna Tozzi, everyone at the 1997 One Yellow Rabbit Summer Lab Intensive, Julien & Friedrich Mayr, and my parents.

I would also like to thank the Alberta Foundation for the Arts and the Alberta College of Art and Design for funding this project in part.

Excerpts from this text have appeared, in earlier form, in *West Coast Line*.

This is a work of fiction and any resemblance to persons living or dead is purely coincidental.

*There she stood, with the waters swirling only a few feet away —
a lumpy figure with a pudding of a face, resolute, unafraid, and
totally confident that she, at sixty-three, could accomplish a feat
that no other human being had managed, and from which
younger and more athletic dare-devils had shrunk. What was she
doing here—a woman of 'refinement' as she constantly reminded
the press—indulging in a common stunt mainly suitable for
exploitation in the music halls that she despised? What Annie
Edson Taylor was doing, as she prepared to enter her barrel,
was to shake her fist at Victorian morality, which decreed that
there was no place but the almshouse for a woman without means
who had reached a certain age.*

— PIERRE BERTON, Niagara: A History of the Falls

Niagara Falls, Canada: Thursday, October 24, 1996: 6:07 A.M.

The first time the sisters visited Niagara Falls, over twenty years ago, they visited like tourists, their arms full of souvenirs, plastic Native dolls, postcards, and they did not need, or want, to hold hands. Whenever they travelled, they did not link hands or arms because they had to hold tightly to their souvenirs or to their raincoats or to their handbags. Efficient, smart travellers. After all, when they went on a cruise around Greece fourteen years ago, Hannelore almost had her bag stolen because she was strolling with her hands free, her arms carelessly uncovered and warmed by the sun.

You should wear the strap over the other shoulder, said Clotilde. Like this. Clotilde's handbag strap over her shoulder like she was carrying a guitar. Held tightly against her body like a pump action shotgun. Hannelore ignored Clotilde and what happened? Bag almost plucked from Hannelore's shoulder like an olive from the branch.

I told you. See? said Clotilde, and Clotilde watched Hannelore put the bag over Hannelore's opposite shoulder the way Clotilde did, strap across Hannelore's breast.

I was going to, said Hannelore. Stop paying so much attention to me and look where you're going. You're about to step in horse shit. There you go.

Not that anything important was in the bags: passports or heart pills in their handbags would be foolish, they wore leather pouches with the important things under their blouses, tucked between their breasts.

Hold hands? They did not need or want to hold hands. In Niagara Falls over twenty years ago, they certainly did not need to hold hands.

(Hannelore had just bought Freddy's record album *Freddy auf hoher See*, Freddy On the High Sea, that year, that's how Hannelore remembers the first visit. A very good record. Such a good singer that Freddy.)

But today, twenty years later, the sisters hold hands so hard Hannelore squeezes Clotilde's knuckles into an untidy wedge-shape.

You're crushing the bones in my hands! yells Clotilde above the roar of the water, the slipping and rushing of the Niagara River.

So Hannelore and Frau Schnadelhuber let go of Clotilde's hands. Frau Schnadelhuber is not a sister, only along for the ride. She does not care if *Freddy auf hoher See* was popular twenty years ago, she left Germany before that. Frau Schnadelhuber is more familiar with "The Hustle" than with the sailing-songs of Freddy and his perfectly kempt 1950s hairstyle and pretty-boy lips. Holding Clotilde's hand is essential to Frau Schnadelhuber. Inadvertently popping Clotilde's knuckles like soapy bubbles.

The crashing and spinning of the Niagara Ball along the rocky floor of the river bed as the Ball nears the precipice. The violent, seat-belted jerking of the women's bodies strapped to the walls inside the huge Ball, the bumps of their sweaty bodies shoved against each other, they swallow each other's air. The grind and lurch and spin of the Ball, the women strapped body to body inside the vessel, through the waves, over the rocks. Sometimes water sweeps over the vessel and if they stretch their necks enough, they can see the Niagara River water, green and murky spitting bubbles, through the tiny window.

My hands, my *hands*, shouts Clotilde again, and again Frau Schnadelhuber and Hannelore let go. Clotilde tries to wring her hands to bring them back from the dead, but their bodies jammed so tightly together leave no room for wringing hands.

Oh Clotilde, moans Frau Schnadelhuber, working her apron between her fingers. I need my cigarettes.

Hold my *wrist* then, says Clotilde. Just don't pull my hand *off*. Hot, I am so *hot*.

4

So Frau Schnadelhuber strangles Clotilde's wrist, or what she thinks is Clotilde's wrist, a panicked handcuff, why does it have to be so dark? And the water sings—a high, murderous song. Obsessive and unrelenting and murderous. Murderous. Such an appropriate word for water that keeps on coming and coming and will keep on coming even after they're dead and their skin is bloated and pocked with underwater maggots.

Murder. A word that purrs like water swirling down the drain.

The soft delicatessen-warm skin of Frau Schnadelhuber pressed into the soft eighty-five-year-old skin of Clotilde pressed into Hannelore's seventy-five-year-old skin in the sour cloud of their breaths.

Hannelore pouts. Hannelore lurches. The restraining-belt across her chest bites into her breasts like her purse did on that cruise fourteen years ago. Hannelore's pout is palpable, like chalky exhaust from a car. Clotilde and Frau Schnadelhuber cough into each other's faces from her pout. Even Hannelore coughs from the smell of her own bad mood.

All right, goddammit Hannelore, yells Clotilde.

Clotilde edges out her fingers to her sister. A jolt bangs her head into Hannelore's helmet. Clotilde's job is to take care of her little sister ever since the war, the command their mother uttered over a bowl of watery turnip pap through lips cracked from malnutrition. Today, the day of their deaths, is no exception, and when Clotilde grabs Hannelore's hand in the dark Clotilde holds on to Hannelore's hand for their mother's dear life. Crammed like too many pickled herrings in a jar, their arms full of nothing but each other and the violent darkness, Frau Schnadelhuber's panicked breaths, and the sound of water. Always the water.

Three women holding hands in the dark like they're eight years old, and not both sides of eighty.

Soft purr of the water that murders right next to the ear. Like a ghost.

She was a childless widow, a teacher, from Bay City, Michigan, plain-looking, weighing one hundred and sixty pounds, aged forty-three without any previous adventures in her life. And then, one day, she decided to go over Niagara Falls in a barrel.

—PERCY ROWE, Niagara Falls & Falls

Germany, 1971

The day Hannelore's daughter-in-law gave birth, Hannelore learned English.

She hummed "Seemann, deine Heimat ist das Meer," Sailor, Your Home is the Sea, and thought about Freddy her favourite Schlager-singer's manly throat as she scribbled on her paper in English so new it shredded the page: My Name is Frau Hannelore Schmitt.

The first English words she wrote on paper, the first English words she ever said out loud in her life. Water, she wrote. The cat. Monday Tuesday Saturday. One two three.

Sree, repeated Hannelore. She wiped her mouth.

Three, said Fräulein Nickel. THHHHHHHH.

Hannelore bragged in church to her many acquaintances about her pregnant daughter-in-law, hopefully it would be a boy, her father always preferred boys, Hannelore also preferred boys. Hannelore would be a grandmother in three months, and hopefully it would be a boy. The other women in her pew nodded in agreement, Yes a boy. Good, a boy.

Frau Drechsel, in the pew in front of Hannelore and Clotilde, peered at Hannelore and said, Instead of making your grand-daughter miserable before she's even born, maybe you should pray she comes out with only one head instead of two.

But it was too late. Hannelore's granddaughter, all the way on the other side of the Atlantic, heard Hannelore, and her eyelids clenched even harder in fury; her hands, curled into fists from the moment she was conceived, punched the hard, dark walls of the uterus in frustration. Would nothing ever change? When she rushed out the vaginal canal, her body lurching over the precipice, she screamed bloody murder at her Oma.

Oh a girl, said Hannelore. She held the telegram in her hand as she got ready for church.

A girl, smirked Frau Drechsel between the hymns.

One two THTHTHree. When Hannelore's granddaughter, Cleopatra Maria Eadburgha, turned three, Frau Drechsel in Hannelore and Clotilde's church contracted pneumonia. Frau Drechsel didn't sit in her pew near the front for so many Sundays, even the gossip died, and Hannelore eventually refused to remember Frau Drechsel ever came to church until Clotilde read the large, black-framed death notice in the paper. Hannelore didn't miss Frau Drechsel's small, currant-red eyes piercing the hard wood of the benches. Two weeks before Cleopatra Maria Eadburgha's fourth birthday.

Died with her boots on, said Clotilde curtly. Frau Drechsel was always one for boots.

Clotilde's arm reached around the paper for her coffee, her fingers thick and meaty. The cool gold rim of the china cup. Clotilde could make a drink cold just by inserting the tip of her index finger in the liquid. An interesting Kaffeeklatsch trick.

Clotilde's hands can give no life, thought Hannelore primly. Spinsters and wasted wombs.

Hannelore drew a breath at Clotilde's coldness regarding the boots, Clotilde's flippance about footwear. Clotilde was sixty-five years old while Hannelore was only fifty-five, and Hannelore slid Clotilde's grouchiness into the cubbyhole of their father's oak desk labelled "old fat fart." Hannelore dabbed her shiny tongue along the edge of the envelope to moisten the glue and pounded the envelope shut with the side of her fist. A birthday card for Cleopatra Maria's fourth birthday. She put the card in the parcel on top of the layers of chocolate-covered marzipan, chocolate-covered Lebkuchen shaped like hearts, and wooden toys tidily wrapped with used crinkled wrapping paper and bound with knotted gold cord left over from Clotilde's sixtieth birthday party. More toys in this parcel than

Hannelore and Clotilde together ever had as children. Brightly painted wooden eggs full of houses and animals, Cleopatra Maria adored eggs, tucked them in the back of her stinky little corduroy pants and pretended to lay them. Such a funny baby. Hannelore tied up the parcel with brown paper and string.

"Cleopatra Maria Schmitt," she wrote on the front, the name so long it went from edge to edge. "KANADA" she wrote and underlined the word twice. Once, Hannelore shortened the name to "Cleopatra." The last time "Maria," a less exotic, more appropriate name. Babies could smother under the wrong name, long names like a cat sitting too long on the face. When she finally accepted the fact that the baby was a girl, Hannelore suggested "Traute," her grandmother's name, for the new baby granddaughter.

Sounds too much like Trout, said Rosario. Kick that idea in the shins.

After the "Maria" birthday card, Rosario, Hannelore's daughter-in-law, smartly replied that the name was Cleopatra Maria, her child would not have Spitznamen; Rosario was never "Rose."

Hannelore rolled her eyes, no one would ever mistake Rosario for a Rose, a beautiful and aromatic flower. No need to worry there.

So Frau Drechsel died of pneumonia. Hannelore and Clotilde sat in the church in their freshly ironed black skirts and every so often Hannelore used her handkerchief to dab an eye. She saw others with their handkerchiefs dabbing their eyes, but not many others, certainly not Clotilde, who didn't cry at anything. Hannelore wondered if there would be eye-dabbing at her own funeral, and freshly ironed skirts. Of course. She wondered if it would also be raining at her funeral. She hoped not. So many funerals these days, Hannelore was getting tired of them. But Hannelore and Clotilde didn't plan to die for a long, long time.

After the funeral service, all the people who attended the funeral went to a restaurant and drank coffee and ate apple cake. Clotilde asked for roll-mops instead and dabbled at the pickled herring

11

with a fork while remembering Frau Henriette Drechsel, bits of pickled onion poking out of Clotilde's mouth like the whiskers of a catfish. Hannelore strained to remember the back of Frau Drechsel's head while she dug through the apple cake, the deep lines around Frau Drechsel's mouth when she sang, the inside of her mouth, the dark interior of her throat like the wet, ribbed inside of a fish. Eyes red like an underwater hog's. The blue and white scarf Frau Drechsel always wore around her wrinkly old hag of a throat. Frau Drechsel, an old family acquaintance now dead, hadn't spoken to them civilly since 1946. Hannelore remembered their falling-out vaguely, something about stealing ration-cards, or no, a potato. Frau Drechsel had accused Hannelore's family of stealing a potato and in the time of the food shortage following the war, this was a very big deal. Hannelore doesn't remember any stolen potato, the only food she remembers is corn, nothing to eat except corn. The ground being dug ready to hold Frau Drechsel, and Hannelore's baby granddaughter four years old in two weeks. And the rain. The rain made things much sadder. Hannelore stayed sad through three cups of coffee and two pieces of apple cake. She licked her index finger and dabbed at the last crumbs on her plate with her finger tip. Frau Drechsel was not that old. Just irritated.

Time for a trip, said Hannelore to Clotilde.

Clotilde nodded, her mouth full. She popped another roll-mop into her mouth and chewed through the flesh of the fish.

The coffee cold and wet like pain in Hannelore's cup.

She lived on the charity of her relatives, but it was given so grudgingly that she decided to have no more of it. For two years she had been obsessed by the problem of money and how to get enough to keep up appearances—for appearances meant a great deal to Annie Taylor. I was always well dressed, she wrote, a member and regular attendant of the Episcopal Church, and my nearest neighbour had not the least idea of where I got my money. . . .

—PIERRE BERTON, Niagara: A History of the Falls

Edmonton, Canada, 1975

After Frau Drechsel's passing, Hannelore and Clotilde visited the family in Edmonton. The greatest shopping mall in North America. Hannelore and Clotilde were the only ones wearing bathing caps, Hannelore and Cleopatra Maria, all of four and a half years old, jumped up and down in time with the waves in the wave pool. Clotilde also jumped in the waves, her bulky spider middle and spindly legs and arms.

Plastic flowers flapped on Hannelore's swimming cap. Flapped and slapped her skull with plastic petals like raw herring falling to the kitchen floor. Strands of white hair straggled from the cap.

Clotilde grimly hopped through the short walls of rolling water. Of course Clotilde was having a wonderful time, although this wave pool was not as good as the wave pools in Germany. Later they would visit toy shops for Cleopatra Maria, the toys badly made plastic and inferior to German-made wooden toys, and drink coffee and eat cake to get their energy back. Canadian cake, spongy and sweet and sickening. Canadian coffee roasted too dark and bitter.

Hannelore kept her breasts covered while she changed—even in front of her granddaughter. Cleopatra Maria skittered around their feet in the dressing room. Noodling up and down the benches and between the rows of lockers, up and down their legs like a busy water beetle.

Hannelore wrestled with Cleopatra Maria's fine, frizzy hair.

This hair is your mother's hair, grumped Hannelore.

No it's my hair, said Cleopatra Maria. Oma, you're doing it *wrong*. Cleopatra Maria's tiny hands scrabbled the air with irritation. She screamed. Because of the hair, because of the nasty sound of her grandmother's voice.

We'll go for some nice cake, said Hannelore as she pulled rhythmically with the comb at the hair on the screaming baby's head, and she snapped Cleopatra Maria's hair into a barrette shaped like a blue rabbit while Clotilde gathered Cleopatra Maria's orange plastic water-wings and toys into a child-sized briefcase. Made in Germany of course. All the best things were, the sisters agreed. Cleopatra Maria would have agreed if they asked her. But of course they didn't ask her. She screamed on.

Outside the pool, Clotilde held one of Cleopatra Maria's hands, Hannelore held the other.

Later, Clotilde carried the tired, noisy baby against her squishy aunty's breasts.

———

How could that be? asked Dieter. That mall and that wave pool weren't put in until the 1980s. Cleopatra Maria would have been almost a teenager.

The fuckings of memory. That must have been a German wave pool and some particularly bad cake, thought Hannelore. Oh well. All wave pools are the same in the end. Stupid and pointless, pseudo-entertainment. She watched Dieter from the step as he gathered leaves from the grass.

She hated it when Dieter was right.

She hated it when he scraped the yard like he was having fun, and almost called out to him, but stopped herself. She stayed standing still calling out to him only in her head because Rosario was sketching her. Rosario liked to sketch. Hannelore liked being sketched.

Germany, 1971

At first missing Dieter was all right. He was at university for such a long time, but it was all right because he was home for holidays. After meeting him at the train station, Hannelore would feed him, put fresh linen on his bed, plump up the cushion in his favourite chair. They laughed at the television together. The same jokes. Sentimental.

Good to have a man in the house again, Heinrich's empty twin bed on the other side of the room—sometimes she would make love to it in her sleep, wake up wet between the between, but with Dieter in the house her mind was occupied, no time for thinking about the empty bed on the other side of the room. Her loneliness for him.

But his move to Kanada with Rosario, an exchange student he met when he was twenty-five, was not all right. Their living together in Germany, then the move to Kanada, then the marriage without a ceremony in Kanada to Rosario, half Mexican, half African, half Chinese, half Kanadian (half mongrel, Hannelore said to herself, only to herself, she would never say this out loud to *anyone*) was worse, and then the baby, not a boy, hopefully the next one would be a boy, the baby her granddaughter who would never live in Germany, never know her heritage, never *christened*, this was a blow to Hannelore's stomach that at first the doctor diagnosed as a violent case of indigestion. Hannelore swallowed bottle after bottle of bitters. Meditated in her yoga class. Swallowed and meditated, but still the pain was there, a gigantic insect burrowing through her intestines. She could not stand Dieter being completely gone. She could not stand being completely alone with only unreliable Clotilde for company.

The doctor agrees that you're killing me, Hannelore screamed into the phone, her back straight and correct.

Don't be an idiot Mutti, Dieter's voice said. Come see the baby. Bring Tante Clotilde. Rosario could use help with the baby.

(Hannelore heard a scrambling on the phone, *I'll* need help with the baby, shrieked Rosario in German and English in the background. What the hell's the matter with *you*!)

Mutti? screeched Rosario into the phone, Hannelore shuddered at the thought of Rosario being linked to her biologically. Mutti indeed.

You should see the baby! shouted Rosario.

Rosario! yelled Hannelore into her bean-green phone. Are you healthy! Are you feeling good!

Mir geht es furchtbar but come anyway! I had to get stitches Cleopatra Maria came barrelling out so fast.

Barrelling, what an odd expression, thought Hannelore, an obviously American, nonsensical expression.

Bring Tante Clotilde, said Dieter's voice.

If I can get her out of Schönbachtal. Pig stubborn.

She's in the nursing home again?

Yes. We had a big fight. Long story, doesn't matter.

Hannelore hung up the phone and unpinned her bathing suit from the clothesline in the basement. Kanada. She and Clotilde had never been to Kanada.

Clotilde. Hannelore would tell Clotilde about their trip to Kanada during their swim. They swam every Sunday, sister and sister cutting slow, identical frog-movements through the water, heads held high above the water like swans'.

We're going to Kanada, said Hannelore, her breath short, droplets of excited water on her lips. You have to move home again so we can get ready.

I've only been at Schönbachtal a week, Clotilde said. But back at Zum Schönbachtal Clotilde began arranging her stockings, knitting needles, and wool back in the suitcase right after coffee and cake. People waiting for visitors who never came lined the walls at

Schönbachtal. The halls smelled of urine. Hannelore couldn't bear Schönbachtal, couldn't bear having a sister in Schönbachtal. Clotilde went to Schönbachtal whenever they had a fight, the nursing home Clotilde's claim to space like it was some kind of hotel.

I'm moving into Schönbachtal for *you*, Clotilde would always say, I am giving you room to think about the stupid things you do.

Hannelore alone in the house with nothing but her feet hammering up and down the stairs for company thinking about her sister in the home, rotting prematurely. Hannelore stood in front of the building, far away from the smell, waiting for Clotilde to click shut her suitcase. Zum Schönbachtal, At The Pretty Creek. Goodbye At The Pretty Creek, hello Kanada.

Niagara Falls, Canada, 1971

Even the first time she saw Niagara Falls, that first visit to Kanada, Hannelore knew that the waterfalls meant everything and nothing. Everything because she was with her son and his little family; nothing because she was with her son and his little family. Her folly and her desire located in her son and the rip in her mother's bosom when he left her for a foreign country, for a wife. Not the same as when Heinrich was killed in the war, but still a loss that seemed almost permanent to her. She wondered what she would do when she got old, and could no longer take care of herself. Would he move back for her? Did he expect her to move from Germany? Sometimes she could swear her womb still missed him, the flesh still trying to conform to his missing shape. But then Cleopatra Maria.

But you can hardly see the water, Hannelore grumbled from the back seat, her back crinkled with pain, her knees stiff as rods. They don't look like in the pictures.

Imagine Rosario claiming the front seat for herself, lying that the back seat made her carsick, while Hannelore had to sit jammed like a squeeze-box in the back. The baby stinking like dirty diapers.

How can I see *any* waterfall with all that mist in the way? Hannelore said.

Rosario looked at Dieter. Hannelore read Rosario's contempt like this morning's newspaper.

Wait, said Dieter.

And the most important thing Hannelore and Clotilde noticed about Kanada on that very first trip was the Falls—Niagara Falls were the only thing they noticed because everything else you could get in Germany and of better quality, but in Germany you could never find these wondrous, monstrous Falls, the bright green old forest and wilderness framing them. The forests were less dense in Germany however. These forests could do with a cleaning.

Monstrous, said Clotilde, baby Cleopatra Maria vomiting peacock blue onto the napkin on Clotilde's shoulder.

Yes, monstrous, said Hannelore.

Hannelore watched the Falls for five minutes that time. Stared at the water rushing and licking over the rim of the cliff, thick on the rocks.

Yes, they are wonderful, said Hannelore, and she had a sad pain in her belly.

We can come back again, said Dieter.

Very nice, sehr schön, said Hannelore asleep, her mind a maple leaf on the surface of the water, slipping over the sleepy edge. A maple leaf like on the Kanadian flag. Yes, she liked Kanada very much. The leaf on the water asleep before the prodigious drop. Maybe liking Kanada was like having an infection. So sleepy.

Hannelore noticed the brown pools of foam frothing on the shores at the bottom of Niagara Falls. She saw the seagulls collected like mosquitoes settle and swim and fly on the water. Dieter told her that some seagulls use projectile vomit as a defence against predators.

We don't really need that information, Dieter, sang out Rosario.

Kanada has such a beautiful landscape, Hannelore said. And what an interesting detail about seagulls. Such a smart boy.

Not *all* seagulls, Mama, said Dieter. Proud of his knowledge.

In the front seat of the car Rosario sneered: "Only if you want to Dieter." Rosario wanted to stab her fingers into her husband's eyes. Rosario could understand the attraction of the water, the overwhelming sight of the water pouring over the edge, the animal roar of the river. But she could not take Mutti's I'm-too-old-to-think-for-myself act. Or how her husband suddenly became ten years old when his mother was in the room. Rosario had seen her mother-in-law crack walnuts apart with her bare hands when Dieter wasn't around. A German Hausfrau thing. Not like Rosario who believed in grabbing the men by the ears and kickin' 'em in the ass.

That time Hannelore and Clotilde's plane tickets said two weeks. They stayed two and a half months. Their first visit to Kanada, Toronto, so exciting, maybe the apartment was a little small for four adults, a healthy baby, and Waldmann the dachshund, but Hannelore did the cooking and cleaning, the apartment needed severe cleaning, the place hurt Hannelore, it was so filthy. Clotilde monitored the laundry, the tonnes of dirty diapers. So she accidentally washed Rosario's red silk brassiere with the diapers, pink a much more festive colour for a baby's bottom, nicht?

And how Rosario *wasted* food. Threw out perfectly good grease, bones with meat and fat still sticking to them, toast crumbs that were more crusts than crumbs. Hannelore and Clotilde had never witnessed such *waste* in their lives.

Dieter and Rosario, mostly Rosario, told them to go back home to Germany. She could take care of the baby fine by herself now.

Don't they have lives? asked Rosario, her hands on her slim hips, slim enough for bright red hip-huggers, pregnancy weight almost entirely gone, her hair in a deliciously frothy afro.

No, said Dieter.

Dieter stirred marble cake batter with a wooden spoon and let Waldmann the dachshund lick flour and grains of sugar from his fingers and bare toes. Marble cake on Sunday afternoon calmed Dieter. Helped him get ready for the week. Dieter hadn't been allowed in the kitchen for two and a half months, Men Not Allowed, said Hannelore. He missed the feeling of batter under his fingernails, Rosario missed the feel of her bare feet on the floor. No Bare Feet In The House, pouted Hannelore's soggy Hausfrau frown.

Rosario wove Kleenexes between her toes and began to paint her toenails "Foxy red." The first chance in two and a half months to paint her nails whatever slutty colour she wanted. She sniffed the fumes from the polish luxuriously. Put her feet up on the kitchen table next to Dieter's bowl of batter and wiggled her toes. After she'd finished her toes, she would start her canvas. The subject would be Hannelore.

She stood five feet four inches in her cotton stockings—a stout and almost shapeless figure in a voluminous black dress, her features fleshy and her greying hair concealed under a broad-brimmed hat. She was determined to make both her fame and her fortune.

—PIERRE BERTON, Niagara: A History of the Falls

Germany, 1916

Hannelore sniffed the steam from the bowl of turnip pap, and doodled in the food with her spoon. She tested the pap, coated the tip of the spoon with pap, touched her tongue to the pap, put her spoon back in the bowl. She blew on the surface. Folded her hands in her lap and hummed to herself, rocked in her little yellow chair, waiting for the pap to cool.

Clotilde stared at Hannelore, Clotilde the older, first-born sister. Clotilde's bowl already licked clean of turnip stew. Clotilde licked her bowl, her spoon, the pot the stew was cooked in, the cooking-spoon that stirred the stew, the fork that mashed the turnips, the knife that sliced them. She gathered up the crumbs of bread from the table and licked them from her palms, she methodically licked the table clean, sometimes crumbs got caught between the cracks, and Clotilde and Hannelore's mother spanked Clotilde, then began to cry hopelessly. Their mother was also hungry. Tired. Clotilde continued to lick through their mother's crying.

What Clotilde really wanted was an egg. She dreamt of the clear smoothness of an egg. There hadn't been eggs for so long, she wanted to eat a hard-boiled egg all by herself, scoop out the crumbly yolk, slither her tongue around the shining white of the egg, break apart the shell and scoop it clean with her tongue. Clotilde wanted more to eat. She wanted more more more. She wanted Hannelore's pap to eat. She grabbed Hannelore's throat with her hands, of course Clotilde got spanked, but the pain didn't matter because it was all in the name of the pap. She knew it was that extra bit of pap that kept her warm when she had to stand in line with the jar at the shop for milk, the adults pushing past her, stand in line for milk that ran out by the time it was her turn to buy. That extra bit of pap kept her from dissolving. Hannelore stood miserably beside Clotilde in those lines. The cold forced Hanne's mouth shut and made her body still.

Too bad if Hannelore had to go hungry. Clotilde was bigger. It was obvious who needed more food.

In the end, their mother interfered. One day, she locked Clotilde out of the sitting room while Hannelore dabbled her way through the small bowl of turnip pap and Clotilde screamed on the other side of the door.

You love Hanne more than you love me, screamed Clotilde, her forehead red and sweating and scrunched with already permanent lines and she only twelve years old.

Hannelore swallowed spoonful after spoonful so slowly, their mother couldn't take the slowness anymore and had to leave the kitchen. She closed the door behind her and stared at Clotilde.

Greedy girl, she said.

Not greedy, screamed Clotilde. Hungry. My body is bigger.

Everyone is hungry, said their mother, But you have always been strong. Your sister is small and she is weak. The strongest have to protect the weakest. You have to protect your sister instead of always stealing from her. One day I won't be around and you will be the only one to take care of her. All she'll have is you and what you choose to give her.

Hannelore opened the kitchen door. Her bowl finally clean of pap. Clotilde stared at Hannelore so hard, Hannelore began to cry.

It's your job to cheer her up when she cries, said their mother to Clotilde. Go do it.

The next day, Clotilde held Hannelore's hand in the cold line-up, shielded Hannelore with her body and her words while the adults trampled around them.

The turnip winter of 1916. The year Clotilde started her job as Hannelore's protector.

But how could that be? said Hannelore. I wasn't born until 1920. And mother never cried. I would remember that. I am also taller than you. I have been for years.

So I shrunk a little, said Clotilde from behind her newspaper. A newspaper from Berlin.

Edmonton, Canada, 1973

Dieter sauntered like he always did, walking with his hips like a hippy, beaded leather cord around his forehead. Owned the world that youngster, but so skinny since he came to Kanada, Hannelore could play the piano on his ribs.

I'm on a diet, he said.

You don't need a diet, said Hannelore.

Yes he does, said Rosario who adored the last word. He eats like a pig.

You look unhealthy! protested Hannelore.

A little German Piglet, said Rosario with Valentine hearts in her voice. She patted Dieter's tummy.

Rosario! said Hannelore.

Dieter took Hannelore and baby Cleopatra Maria to the German delicatessen in the mall. The family moved from Toronto to this crappy little city for Dieter's job when Cleopatra turned eighteen months. A Bavarian delicatessen. What a disappointment, Hannelore so looked forward to speaking German with other Germans and the only other Germans available were Bavarians.

But the waitresses and cooks in the Dirndl dresses, the music piped through the speakers—navy marches from the twenties and schmalz folk-songs—drew Hannelore. She and Clotilde had been in Edmonton for only one week now, were already getting a little edgy, feeling under-appreciated by the family that's what, and the customers with the feathers in their hats threw out sticky, shiny mental threads that pulled at Hannelore's eyelids and body like fish hooks, dragged her to the main counter, the smell of fifteen kinds of sausages, freshly fried Bauern Schnitzel, stewed red cabbage and potato salad with small bits of bacon steaming in deep metal pans. Packages of Lebkuchen, Mozart Kugeln, and Glücks-Käfer.

The waitresses' voices pure, clean water fizzing in the glass of Hannelore's brain.

Real food, sighed Hannelore as she pointed at a large and juicy blood sausage.

Good food, sighed Hannelore, the clang of pans full of plump Bratwurst ready for her to put her mouth around.

Made by Bavarians, Hannelore sighed, and she folded her hands over her purse while the Bavarians wrapped up the slices of dry, Hungarian salami, Rosario's favourite.

All? asked the woman behind the counter, her hair in braided balls on both sides of her head like she'd just stepped out of a Hummel painting. "Frau Schnadelhuber" said her name-tag. Accented Southern German that Hannelore could cut with a knife and spear with a fork and bury in creamed horseradish.

Hannelore's husband was a Southerner. So what if he was Bavarian. She could see the man behind the Bavarian. Light contempt for people from the South. She remembered reading an article in *Spiegel* magazine titled, Are Bavarians Stupid? and even though her husband was Bavarian she had to agree that Bavarians in general were maybe not stupid but certainly different, or sometimes just not very clean. Her husband the exception of course. She never said out *loud* that Bavarians were different, but she thought about their difference often, and here in the delicatessen, these women behind the counter certainly talked like they were from a different part of Germany and looked *very* different in those dresses which weren't even *accurate*, but some kind of German-American costumed mishmash covered with butcher's aprons. Women wearing feathered hats? Although her husband wasn't always serious enough and sometimes his kidding annoyed her. But then, light contempt had always been Hannelore's flashlight in the dark. Bavarians were silly, but they were the only Germans in this very little Kanadian town and she would come back to this delicatessen with Clotilde several more times for Mittagessen.

In the car on the way back, Hannelore did imitations of Bavarians, imitations of the woman named Frau Schnadelhuber while Dieter drove. Grüss Gott, she mimicked, grinding the g's in the back of her throat like she was about to spit up an entire blood sausage.

Grüss Gott, mimicked Cleopatra Maria, her very first words, this baby a genius, the first words out of her mouth. A child after Hannelore's own heart. When they got home, Hannelore would give the baby an extra large piece of cake to scream about.

In 1942, a War Bond sales drive was conducted across New York State with effigies of Hitler, Mussolini and Hirohito riding in a "Bondmobile." . . . [A]s five thousand persons cheered, the effigies were placed in a wooden boat, doused with gasoline, set ablaze and released into the rapids just above the American Falls.

—ANDY O'BRIEN, Daredevils of Niagara

Niagara Falls, Canada: Thursday, October 24, 1996: 5:56 A.M.

Prosit, they say on shore before entering the vessel, the shining air cold as hell and dawn barely there. Cleopatra Maria is with them, and will be on the shore at the bottom, she says, to greet them when they get out and help them get the Niagara Ball back in the truck so they can go to the hotel and enjoy the rest of their holiday. Frau Schnadelhuber wants to try out the casino. When they have set off in the Ball, Cleopatra Maria will alert an ambulance, but not the police. The ambulance will call the police anyway.

Hannelore isn't confident about Cleopatra Maria driving the truck, Cleopatra Maria seems a little too eager to get behind the huge steering wheel in the truck, like this is all *fun*. Cleopatra Maria (call me Patty she says, but no one ever does) pulls out a bottle of champagne and four plastic cups from the trunk of the station wagon, she used up all of this week's allowance, twenty-six years old and still getting allowance yes she knows this is pathetic, and the Sekt froths into the glasses like the water at the bottom of Horseshoe Falls where the twisting mist births to shoot hundreds of feet up into the air. Cleopatra Maria looks so young, Hannelore is surprised anyone in a liquor store would even let her in the front door, let alone sell her a bottle of champagne. Even in Alberta Cleopatra Maria is asked for identification, Hannelore would ask Cleopatra Maria for identification if Hannelore didn't know her. Not like Germany, where everyone is of legal drinking age—German beer more nourishing than water.

Frau Schnadelhuber is disappointed she doesn't have beer for her Sekt, her favourite drink is Sekt and beer together. Hannelore would have preferred a Malteser over Sekt, but good for Cleopatra, Sekt is more bracing, more symbolic, than Malteser. They should have brought another bottle to smash against the side of the vessel.

Ah but then the broken glass. Who would pick up the broken glass? Hannelore wouldn't have time to pick up the broken glass, Cleopatra Maria could pick up the shards but would miss pieces. Hannelore would need damp paper towels for the shards. Good thing there wasn't another bottle to smash, and the waste, what a stupid idea to bring a second bottle, thought Hannelore. Good thing they didn't let Hannelore loose in the liquor store. Cleopatra Maria is a gift of a girl, Hannelore's face flushes with pride at her beautiful and studious granddaughter who helped get them all this way.

Why aren't you guys drinking? demands Cleopatra Maria. You don't like it? I used up my whole allowance to buy this stupid bottle! Jesus!

Clotilde is happy with her glass of Sekt so soon after her morning coffee, she has never been a picky woman, and she licks a spilled drop wandering down her chin with an amphibian's tongue.

Prosit, say the four women again, and clink their cups, all in tears. Sentimental. Hannelore certainly in the most tears of all, except for Clotilde of course who doesn't cry about anything because Clotilde thinks she's a man. Frau Schnadelhuber has seen enough men cry in her time so she is glad about Clotilde's gaunt, dry cheeks, the wide smile distorting Clotilde's face. So all the women cry except for Clotilde, and Hannelore cries the hardest because going over Niagara Falls in a space-age barrel is her idea, after all. This is the best explanation for why the tears run so thickly down her face from her eyes and her nose and into her handful of Kleenex. The Niagara River water slides over the cliff as though the liquid in their tears has no connection to the liquid bubbling and screaming over the rocks in the ancient river bed.

No connection whatsoever.

Hannelore prays a little to the foaming Sekt in her cup, the spill of foam over the plastic edge, over her fingers. Her fingers will be sticky and sugary. She feels drunk just from the smell of the drink.

A toast to Annie Edson Taylor, Hannelore says suddenly, loudly.

Who? says Clotilde.

The first person to go over Niagara Falls in a barrel, says Cleopatra Maria. Don't you remember anything? Why is it taking you guys so long to drink? I don't think you like the champagne. I think you hate it. I don't know why I bother trying to be nice.

The crazy nut in her ridiculous barrel, says Frau Schnadelhuber, swirling the champagne around in her cup. Just like us.

This barrel is *much* more efficient than Annie Edson Taylor's! says Cleopatra Maria. I've done the calculations!

All right, says Clotilde. Prosit! A toast to that crazy woman Annie and to crazy us.

Save me a place at your table Frau Taylor, Hannelore says quietly. Prosit, she whispers and cries so hard she snorts. Anna Edson Taylor. The Queen of the Mist. Then Hannelore drinks the Sekt quickly because she knows it will taste terrible. Hannelore knows from working for ten years as an usher-bartender that young people like Cleopatra Maria always prefer Sweet Shit champagne.

This champagne is delicious! says Frau Schnadelhuber and Cleopatra Maria blushes.

After the three women are secured in the Niagara Ball, some friendly tourists in turbans and bright saris and ties will see Cleopatra Maria struggling with the Ball and help her roll it into the water, then they will carry on their early morning tourist way.

In her grave, Annie Edson Taylor's bones shift. A little to the north.

The Royal Auditorium, Canada, 1995

Because of the funerals. This is how Hannelore would always answer.

Then she would arrange the glasses on the counter and pour in the wine. Half the glasses full of red, half full of white. Check to make sure there was enough ice for highballs and pop. Hannelore prided herself on her bartending efficiency. The women at the Royal Auditorium where Hannelore worked always wanted to know why she moved to Canada. That's far away, they'd say, as though she didn't know that. Of course Hannelore knew Germany was far away. That was the point.

I had to go to three funerals in one day, said Hannelore. I couldn't make it to all three of them and I couldn't decide which one to miss. All I know is I had to go to all three, two acquaintances from when I was a girl, one a friend of my mother's. And there was no one left in the world I liked. A world war and then old age don't leave many likeable people behind.

Yes but still, someone would say, probably Dot. Dot and Hannelore always worked the third floor bar together.

At Ilse's funeral I had enough, said Hannelore, and she would sit back, ready to tell her story.

Hannelore was not Ilse gathering overblown roses in the garden at the seniors' lodge, the blossoms trembling in Ilse's hands so hard the petals started to drop. Light plunks on the ground between Ilse's and Hannelore's orthopaedic-shod feet.

But these roses are dead, said Hannelore gently. You should cut the new, tight ones.

But the smell is always the best just before they die, said Ilse.

And the smile on Ilse's tiny, wrinkled face, her eyes deep behind the thick, thick lenses of her glasses. Ilse a long-ago friend of her and Clotilde's mother's. Body fragile like a bird's the nurses used to say. Hannelore will forever hate this comparison of old women to birds.

When I'm not wearing my glasses and I look at the moon, Ilse once told Hannelore, there are four moons arranged like a clover-leaf. The thought of a clover-moon caught in Hannelore's stomach, invaded her intestines, made her choke back vomit and over-whelming, supremely irritating tears.

Cataracts, Dot would interrupt. Makes you see four moons. My Bob had a cataract operation.

Hannelore would ignore Dot. Hannelore did not care about Bob's cataracts, especially in the middle of the story.

Enough! Hannelore slammed down a large cooking-pan in her head. Ilse's death was the last death and she had had enough of death. Her brain was a crumbling white roll. Too many deaths, too many sick women, too many dead husbands, too many funerals and people not in their proper seats in the congregation. Too many stones in her garden, her garden grew *stones* instead of flowers, too many dead flowers.

Hannelore had years left, she was not old, she had survived World War II, and Ilse was not old and had survived *both* World Wars but now Ilse was dead. But now young Hannelore was buried by the past, the chairs in her house in exactly the same positions as where her grandfather set them a hundred years ago. The pictures on the walls in positions identical to when Hannelore was born, then Dieter was born. The same pictures, the same places. Every-thing the same except that there were no children in the house, no one to take care of her except for Clotilde if Hannelore became ill, and Clotilde was nearly ten years older, no guarantee that she would be around for Hannelore. Not like when they took care of their father until he died, not like when their mother took care of *her* father, their grandfather, until he died. There was no one left. Everything the same, but the roses Hannelore's father planted were overrun by aphids, dissolving into pocked syrup. The garden that shot up gravestones instead of irises. Hannelore was tired of irises. Who chose the irises in the first place? In her heart, she craved not flowers, but her boy and his Kanadian maple trees.

So Ilse was dead and Hannelore's head was too warm. Hannelore and Clotilde stumped past the headstones in the Friedhof, the square plots, some so fresh the stones hadn't even been laid yet. Others, plaques, so old the grass crawled over them, young men killed in the wars, some as young as sixteen, sons of her neighbours. When she and Clotilde were girls, Clotilde pushed Hannelore out of swings, into closets, down stairs for fun, until their mother commanded Clotilde to take care of Hannelore. Now Hannelore cannot bear the thought of being pushed into a graveyard. Or taking her turn to push her older, fragile sister into the earth.

Clotilde and Hannelore walked to all the funerals, overtired themselves and, on the way home, Hannelore hooked one of her shoes between two cobblestones, cobblestones hard on the feet, hard on the knees, and fell in the square by the Rathaus. She clung to the side of the stone fountain and swore.

The freezing-cold water in the fountain reflecting green on Hannelore's skin.

Goodbye Ilse. The tired romance of overblown roses. The remains of Ilse's clover-moon flavours trapped in Hannelore's mouth.

Clotilde's eyes draped by the wrinkled folds of her eyelids, her lips tight, her hair cut straight across the back of her neck like the blade of an axe, but Clotilde and her cane nothing like an axe, trying to help Hannelore up from the gritty stones, trying to hold on to her cane and her purse and Hannelore all at the same time.

I'll do it myself, said Hannelore. I don't want you falling too.

Hannelore's fall, the clash of pots falling to the floor in her head.

No time, said Clotilde.

The next morning they swam side by side in the pool, their capped heads up, their arms circling like the moving hands of a clock, but Hannelore's grief would not wash away.

Hannelore decided they would go live with Dieter. Time for a trip. A long one.

No, I'm not coming, said Clotilde. Don't even dream about it. If you bother me anymore I'll move into Schönbachtal for good.

The sisters would sleep in Cleopatra Maria's room, this is what they did every time they visited. Hannelore would help Dieter and Rosario rent a bigger house with her savings and her widow's pension.

Forget it, said Clotilde. Not interested.

But you'll be all alone, said Hannelore.

Clotilde swam a few centimetres ahead, small waves from her stroking arms washing into Hannelore, Clotilde's straggly grey hairs leaking from the pink rubber bathing cap. Hannelore watched the blue strips of Clotilde's bathing suit moving under the water, smelled the chlorine.

Dot said, But of course she came with you.

Of course, said Hannelore.

That's good, said Dot.

I moved to Canada because of the wilderness, said Hannelore. This is how she would answer at other times. Usually when a customer at the Royal Auditorium asked her about her accent.

The wilderness of course, Hannelore would repeat.

The happiest day of her life was when Dieter and Rosario gave her a muskrat fur coat, an outrageous, wonderful coat made in Kanada. She put it on in front of them and felt like an empress.

Now you won't be so cold when you come to visit, said Rosario.

Hannelore walked around the living room in the coat, felt the shiny brown lining of the coat fuse with her skin.

Where will I wear this? I have no place to wear a coat like this.

Wear it here when you visit in the winters so you won't be cold, said Dieter.

I just said that, said Rosario.

Hannelore smiled at Dieter, then stared pointedly at Rosario's bright red toenails on Rosario's bare bare feet.

Hannelore wore her coat to the delicatessen. She bundled into one of the tiny booths with her tray of Bauern Schnitzel with potato salad and Sauerkraut and her coat and after she set out Cleopatra Maria's plate of food, began to eat like a bear. Cleopatra Maria, not even six years old, but already reading the entire newspaper by herself every day sat at the table with the newspaper spread out messily on the bench beside her. "Das ist die Liebe der Matrosen," That is the Love of the Sailor, trumpeted from the speaker in the corner above their heads.

You look like a Saskvutsch Hannelore, said Clotilde from across the table. "Sasquatch" a new Kanadian word she found in the paper. What the hell is this Saskvutsch? asked Clotilde and Rosario explained to her about big feet.

You look like a Saskvutsch, said Clotilde and she laughed a laugh as dry as the desert. Cleopatra Maria spilled a bit of milk on the business section of her newspaper and began to scream. Clotilde sipped the last of her coffee from her cup, good coffee considering they were in Kanada, and looked around for a waitress to give her more.

Guten Tag, Frau Schnadelhuber! Clotilde called, and the Bavarian labelled Frau Schnadelhuber poured more coffee into Clotilde's cup. Clotilde's face cracked into a smile.

Frau Schnadelhuber looked through her spectacles at Clotilde, at the screaming Cleopatra Maria, and at Hannelore's coat. Frau Schnadelhuber had seen stranger things. The owner of the delicatessen was stranger than the coat—Frau Schnadelhuber and everyone who worked at the delicatessen worked for a Madame in Los Angeles who, sentimental for the old country, ran this delicatessen tucked as far away from L.A. as possible. Her little secret. They said the Madame ran the delicatessen and her many brothels from her bed and did nothing but talk on the phone and eat Mozart balls and marzipan shaped like pigs all day. The stupid Northern German woman with her crazy accent in the oversized fur coat was nothing unusual, thought Frau Schnadelhuber. Frau Schnadelhuber poured coffee like bordello owners were just another kind of horseradish.

Nice coat, said Frau Schnadelhuber, and she and Clotilde raised their eyebrows at each other.

Frau Schnadelhuber left them to get more coffee. She could smell the Wiener Schnitzel had been frying too long.

Hannelore wore the coat when the family drove to the mountains, her coat fit in with the mountains and the trees, so well dressed.

She wanted to take it with her into the pool area at the hot springs, but the clerks wouldn't let her. She couldn't enjoy the water in the springs because she was so concerned about the coat.

Hannelore wore it every time she went to the delicatessen to show off in front of those other Germans, but Hannelore never took it back to Germany with her. Too much space in the luggage. Too pretentious.

I immigrated to Canada because of the coat, said Hannelore. I could tell my son and his wife wanted me to come live with them. My son was crying for his Mama's help. I could not say no.

That's a very interesting story, the customer would say and then hightail it down the lobby to the exit door.

Because of Clotilde. This is how Hannelore would answer when she asked herself why she moved to Canada and became a landed immigrant.

Hannelore's baby granddaughter ten years old, had not written her Oma or her Tante *once* that year, not even to say thank you for the Christmas money and presents. Clotilde hunched over the breakfast table, her bony shoulders poking through the cardigan, chewing her Muesli and yogurt, teeth like a horse Clotilde had, smacking the cereal loudly but Hannelore's faulty hearing aid sat on top of the cabinet. Hannelore watched Clotilde's lips smack her cereal, suck from her coffee cup with the withered lips of a chimpanzee, the glisten of Clotilde's saliva on the bottom lip as she sucked again at the cup. Clotilde's movements slow but precise, the knobbly bones in her fingers, the gross green veins on the backs of Clotilde's hands under the peppering of brown spots and sagging skin.

Everything Clotilde did nowadays was slow. Clotilde dried the dishes with Hannelore slowly, didn't even dry them completely but this didn't matter because she took so long with the dishcloth, the air had time to dry the wet dishes between her hands. So big and strong Clotilde used to be. Beating other girls and smaller boys to bloody piles, carrying huge pails of milk, bags of corn. A tank of a woman. Like the American tank that drove through the hedge in 1945. Looking at Clotilde in the old days, you couldn't help thinking: Venison Ragout with Spätzle. A hearty dish.

Now Clotilde looked more like Turnip Pap. Clotilde's hair stood up in a grey spiky fringe around her forehead.

You don't eat enough, said Hannelore. Have another Brötchen with this nice plum compote. Here is some Quark to put on top.

Na, grumbled Clotilde behind her paper. A newspaper from Frankfurt.

Hannelore put the breakfast things on the tray. Clotilde stood up slowly from her chair, grasped the edge of the table with her bony hands. Clotilde scooped the crumbs from the tablecloth into the palm of her hand and clumped to the kitchen in her heavy black shoes.

Hannelore watched Clotilde's slowness. Turned with the loaded tray to the kitchen.

We are rotting here, Hannelore said loudly.

What were you staring at? asked Clotilde, the dish towel in her hand ready for the wet plates.

We should get a dishwasher, said Hannelore. Wash and dry these stupid dishes and get it over with.

You still have to wash the dishes before they go in. Double the work.

You're right, said Hannelore.

Clotilde dried a fork slowly, one tine at a time.

But you don't have to dry them, said Hannelore watching the air dry the fork between Clotilde's hands. The machine dries them.

I like to dry dishes. Calming, said Clotilde.

Calming for you, thought Hannelore.

What were you staring at? asked Clotilde. Did I have food on my face?

I was thinking about how we rot.

Thinking. You're not good at thinking, Hannelore. Such morbid thoughts, how we rot.

Clotilde walked slowly to the utensil cupboard, put the fork in the drawer, walked back to the sink.

I need my cane today, Clotilde said. Stiff all over.

Tomorrow afternoon they would fly to Kanada for their annual visit. The ticket said three weeks, they planned three weeks. This time the sisters would only stay six weeks.

That evening across the table strewn with presents they would take with them to Kanada tomorrow—whole salami sausages for

46

Rosario tucked into umbrella cases to trick customs, high-waisted underwear in plastic packages for Dieter, chocolate eggs for Cleopatra Maria—Hannelore saw white sleep collected in the corners of Clotilde's eyes, like the way sleep used to be in their father's eyes, in Frau Drechsel's eyes. The decorations of age.

Wipe your eyes! said Hannelore. Put down that paper for one stinking second and wipe your eyes.

Clotilde's eyes moist and sagging.

Wipe your own! retorted Clotilde.

Hannelore lifted up her glasses and dabbed her index finger at the corner of her eye. White stuff like in old people's eyes. Rheumy, tired eyes. She wasn't old.

Hannelore stood up to latch the window and stop the cold air from blowing through. Wipe your own. Those words made her sad. She did not have time to waste being sad.

But tomorrow they would be on a plane to Kanada. Hannelore would watch Clotilde in Kanada, drying the forks as she picked them from the dishwasher, and she would think, Time for a trip.

Actually, the only living creature known to have survived this drop is said to have been a female bull terrier whose irritated and sadistic owner dropped it into the current in November, 1856, from the Goat Island Bridge. The terrier was found on shore the following spring; it had survived the winter by eating a dead cow that had been swept over the Falls and kept preserved by the intense cold.

—ANDY O'BRIEN, Daredevils of Niagara

Niagara Falls, Canada, 1980

The second time Hannelore saw Niagara Falls, by accident, by night, she was by herself.

She was on her way to live with Dieter and Rosario and Cleopatra Maria, now almost ten, in Edmonton, that crappy city on the other side of the country nowhere near Niagara Falls. Clotilde was still in Germany, in their house, stewing in her own juice alone, cursing what their mother had made Clotilde promise.

Of course Hannelore knew that Clotilde would follow. Several months later. Clotilde could not stand being alone.

Hannelore booked a one-way ticket and packed one suitcase. She put her most important things, photo albums and her china cup collection, in boxes wrapped with brown paper, and had them picked up and shipped to meet her in Kanada. Underlined twice. Tablecloths. Her mother's silver and her father's portrait. Clothing.

Her mother's picture. 1906. Her husband Heinrich. 1940. Home from the war. She sent a letter to him every day in her head, and another letter every day to her mother, telling them to expect her imminent arrival. These were not suicide notes, just reservations for her seat at the table, and to remind them that she still didn't like turnips.

Delicately trapped under the surface of the photographic paper. Her mother's large brown eyes that magically reappeared in Cleopatra Maria's brown face. The quiltings of human flesh.

Hannelore didn't get back on the plane during the stopover in Toronto, left her most comfortable house shoes on board by accident because she wanted to see Niagara Falls. What she loved the most about Kanada besides her son's family was Niagara Falls, a shame they moved away from that part of the country, and it took her half a day with her crappy and impatient English to find out how to take a bus to the Water. To the gentle sliding of the Water over the edge of the cliff.

On the bus, fumes blew in the open door and she choked, the exhaust gave her a headache so she took a pill, but fumes were not the important thing. The bus-drivers yelled at each other about hot dogs, she understood the word "hot dogs" and here she was in Kanada, but not with her son. The squeak of the windshield wipers, the whirr of the motor as the bus left the station. "Nous parlons français & wir sprechen Deutsch." This was the hotel where she would stay. Coughs and snorts from other passengers, and a slick black road. Trees bare or orange from the autumn.

The bus driver helped Hannelore down the steps of the bus, she clutched his arm on the way down, the strong muscles beneath his shirt.

Need help finding a cab? he asked.

What? she asked.

Help? Taxi?

No, she said.

Nutty old ladies. Nutty German tourists.

She walked along River Road, her feet and fat old ankles along the river, she mourned her ankles, the mounds of orange, soggy North American maple leaves, the pools of autumn rainwater. The dark green of the river, green like khaki, and once there were three funerals, three, and she went to all of them and in the process her black ironed skirt almost became her uniform forever. She hated dressing in black. The fabric of mourning stuck to her skin like a toxic smell. Of course she would die, Clotilde too, but not like that, not with that *smell* enveloping their bodies. Embalming fluid.

She walked slowly and the mist from the Falls was far away, but no matter, she was used to walking up the gigantic hill on Pieper Strasse and around her village on Kirchberg Strasse. Sometimes at home she walked for an hour and a half; her doctor told her this was good for her and then she came home and fell asleep before even sitting down, she was so tired.

The back of her neck felt cold from the wet. Silver gobs of standing binoculars along the path. She stopped and peered into one of the dark holes. Her glasses banged on the metal of the binoculars.

Seagulls gathered and flew over the water near the bottom of the Falls.

Waiting for the remains, she thought. Projectile vomit, she thought distastefully.

The green and then the rim and then the wind. From where she was all she could see was the column of mist, the giant spectre.

She leaned on the bannister above where the water curved over the edge, the same spot she stood last time, the baby screaming over her shoulder. Except this time she stood for an hour, her legs stiff, her hair only lightly disordered under the plastic rain-cap. Another woman stood farther down the railing from Hannelore, her face hidden by a sweeping feather on her hat except for the woman's jowl which reminded Hannelore of a Dr. Oetker lemon pudding. The hem of the woman's long skirt spattered with mud. Hannelore never knew how cold and heavy and wet water could be. A soggy evening gown. The soaked, cream-coloured satin of her wedding gown clinging to her skin and dragging her to the ground. The woman and her jowl and her muddy skirt walked away upriver. Hannelore was glad. She wanted the view to herself.

Three funerals, four five six, six thousand, six million, eighteen billion.

Not water but grey light, twirling clouds of mist.

Clotilde! she called. She leaned over the curled metal rails and sucked in all the water she could with her eyes.

Her voice fell into the river and slid over the edge.

Holy Jesus, sighed Hannelore. She rubbed her hands all over her face, she died for sleep on the bus, sleep a heavy blanket that rustled around her body. The bus from Niagara Falls to Edmonton rumbled on, chasing the setting sun.

That was the second visit to Niagara Falls. When she finally arrived in Edmonton, Hannelore knew she was getting old when her baby boy barked at her with a mouth surrounded with grey whiskers like a dog's, barking loudly and insistently because he thought she'd gone completely deaf not to mention stupid for deliberately missing her plane.

But buses are easier, said Hannelore. I don't like gigantic airports. Besides, you shouldn't have moved so far away from Niagara Falls, said Hannelore. Such a wonderful landscape.

While Dieter yelled at her, she hummed "Seemann deine Heimat ist das Meer" and started to iron the red and white dishcloths she'd brought with her. Her initials embroidered in red thread in the corners.

On that bus, when she finally fell asleep, she dreamed that she and Clotilde were wearing long beautiful gowns and feathered hats and floating like balloons among the seagulls. They were dressed in black velvet beaded with water drops, their skirts full like balloons, and then she woke up, her face slick with sweat, her lips dry and caked with old spit.

She lied about her age, admitting to forty-two years, believing the press would prefer a younger woman to make the plunge. Some journalists went along with the charade. One described her as "agile, athletic and strong"; another said she cut a sturdy, graceful figure. But others, more sceptical, put her age at fifty. She was thirteen years older than that.

—PIERRE BERTON, Niagara: A History of the Falls

Niagara Falls, Canada: Thursday, October 24, 1996: 6:08 A.M.

Oma? thinks Cleopatra Maria. Cleopatra Maria has never driven a truck alone before, never one so high above the ground, although she's been driving since she was ten years old, the only kid on her block allowed to drive that young. Her little bum sitting high up on pillows and the seat-belt snapping every so often into her forehead. Here she is driving too high, looking for a phone to call an ambulance which she *knows* they will not need. She *knows* it, she got an A in physics and the vessel is indestructible, her Oma and Tante and Frau Schnadelhuber safely coccooned in a giant foam-interior egg. But Cleopatra Maria's nerves are shot like an alcoholic's. She is no less

The bumping and rolling will surely break their skulls even with the helmets, thinks Hannelore, and Frau Schnadelhuber in her Dirndl dress, skirt practically flipped up over her head. Who would wear such clothing on an expedition like this? Perpetually in a Dirndl. Not even a real Dirndl Kleid but an L.A. Madame's version of a Dirndl.

Frau Schnadelhuber said, Me, I'm getting too old for this bullshit, okay. I'm too old to be tricked up like Heidi all the time, but that job was my life. This uniform is my skin, okay?

And Hannelore has to admit she understands. Hannelore should have worn her own usher uniform maybe. Hannelore, Clotilde, and Frau Schnadelhuber breathe into each other's faces, the champagne on shore a nice, symbolic gesture, but their breaths have turned sour because of the alcohol and fear drying their tongues. Smells like a than an accomplice. If they die, she will be the only one left, the only one responsible. Being fluent in five languages won't help her a whole lot when she's sorting underwear in the prison laundry. Maybe she should get a tattoo now to make her look tougher to the other inmates.

911. Nine-one-one, the two one-ones spelled out as ones instead of eleven as in seven-eleven because in an emergency people would try to dial eleven and of course wouldn't find eleven on the phone. Is it 911 in Niagara Falls too? Of course, what a silly thought. Cleopatra Maria is only twenty-six years old after all, although she has been in university for ten years already and can speak five languages

distillery. Smells like a stable. Jolts and jerks, the harnesses keep them from splattering against the fortified glass, like Greek salad on the inside of a windshield. Hannelore has never been overly fond of vegetables, Canadians *never* put enough dressing or sugar in their salads. Synthetic oils. Hannelore has always hated seat-belts. She would like to disconnect this one *now*.

I think if I have to drown, this is the way to do it, gasps Frau Schnadelhuber, Better this than alone in a nursing home or a hospital.

We're not going to drown, we're going to break records, says Hannelore.

And the law, gasps Clotilde.

What are they going to do, Clotilde? shouts Frau Schnadelhuber, Give us life sentences?

The women laugh, and Frau Schnadelhuber suddenly feels merry.

You should have been a comedienne Friedl, says Clotilde.

It never occurred to Hannelore that Frau Schnadelhuber had a first name. Friedl. An inappropriately poetic name for a waitress. But Hannelore could never call Frau Schnadelhuber "Friedl." That would mean they were friends, that would mean Hannelore approved of Clotilde's and Frau Schnadelhuber's friendship. Oh well. She supposes the fluently, and can write both Latin and ancient Greek.

Yes, her social skills have suffered from educational acceleration but boys her age are next door to useless anyway, it only makes evolutionary sense, and maybe her prodigious brains and slightly oversized cranium are why her best friends are all seventy-five or older.

She will use the other ninety percent of her brain to tap her telepathic powers and communicate with her Oma in the vessel.

Uh-oh. The German telepathic power lines seem to be down. All she can think of is French.

Grandmère! Cleopatra Maria screams.

day of her death is better than no day at all for turning over a new relationship leaf. Hannelore smiles at Frau Schnadelhuber and her feelings are not a little hurt at Frau Schnadelhuber's shocked expression.

Grandmère? thinks Hannelore.

The Niagara Ball suddenly crashes to a stop so violently Hannelore's mouth makes a perfectly round O and her hands try to fly to her mouth but Frau Schnadelhuber's and Clotilde's bodies pin her arms to her sides. Frau Schnadelhuber and Clotilde suspended just above her, pinned to the walls and sweat from Frau Schnadelhuber's chin drips onto Hannelore's cheek. Hannelore nearly vomits. And here she is without a Kleenex in sight.

The Niagara Ball—eerily motionless. Still the sound of water. Hannelore feels like a giant omelette.

But where are we? says Hannelore, I don't understand.

Hannelore's heart in her mouth, she chews frantically, her heart is made of chewing gum sticking to her dentures because she knows the Ball is stuck, the windshield fogged up with their breath

Janitor Alvarez in his yellow work slicker jumps over the barrier and pokes furiously at the giant orange egg with his broom. A giant egg freakishly lodged in one of the tunnel openings behind the Falls, he kicks and pushes it, bangs it with his fist and prods it with his elbows, the cement floor slippery with water from the Falls and full of garbage, tourists treat the tunnels like a Mexican beach. Yes, the garbage keeps him working, but this does not mean he is not sick to death of garbage garbage garbage as persistent as all the goddamn water, just keeps on coming and never the end, that final trickle that means he can go home and never see another tourist's mess

but she sees only the colour of water, where is the sky? Stuck somewhere behind the Falls, they couldn't be as far as the whirlpool yet, and the nightmare has come true, she tempted Providence and now they will die of asphyxiation, Hannelore will drown in her sister's halitosis and this wasn't the way it was supposed to be, dead with lesbians, yes she's finally said the word, admits her eighty-five-year-old sister probably isn't going through a phase, she's known it ever since that terrible time in the war when Hannelore caught Clotilde kissing and hugging and kissing that, that *woman*.

I was just getting a fish bone out of her throat, said Clotilde, her arm still around the girlfriend.

There was fish for dinner and you didn't save me any? blurted Hannelore. And then she realized Clotilde's lie.

When they were young, Clotilde always assumed Hannelore was especially stupid and useless and had no trouble showing it. The family hadn't eaten fish in years.

But now is no time for flashbacks.

Hannelore listens to the violent banging of rocks on the outside of the vessel, the sound terrifies her, she is afraid of the exterior getting punctured, she is terrified, she is terrified.

ever, ever again. And here is just one more giant piece of garbage buggering up his tunnels and making his life a trial. He works too hard to have his good work undone by North American slobs.

Water spurts and jets around the giant ball onto Janitor Alvarez, down his collar and into his bum crack. Always the big joke that his first name is really Janitor. A joke his father played on him his whole life. His father a special bastard.

Bastard! shouts Janitor Alvarez and he levers the giant ball of garbage out with the broom stick and a furious double kick. The giant egg pops from the tunnel, a cork from a giant bottle of tart champagne.

Hannelore will never forgive herself for killing not only her sister but also Frau Schnadelhuber, no no, Friedl, in her ridiculous Heidi uniform, her feathered hat pinned to her head. She refused to wear a helmet. That dress and that hat make Hannelore want to cry. Hannelore *hates* to cry.

A terrible jerk and Hannelore, Clotilde, Frau Schnadelhuber scream so hard their vocal cords almost snap. They scream for their lives.

Janitor bounces backwards onto his ass, the hard wet concrete, the pools of freezing shitty water. One slip and he could have been seagull hors d'oeuvre on the rocks below. He stands up, straightens the socks in his rubber boots.

Volare, he hums, and jumps back over the barrier.

Grandmère! screams Cleopatra Maria, crying wildly because she can't find number eleven on the touch-tone phone.

The paramedics will slap a brown paper bag over her nose and mouth to stop her hyperventilating. Then they will unfurl the body-bags.

The dull white curtain of water. Not water. Nathan T. Boya in his Plunge-o-Sphere didn't even know he'd gone over the Falls until the police pulled him over to shore and fined his daredevil's ass off. Hannelore will never understand the depth of that water, the privacy and coolness in those giant waterfalls surrounded by human tricks and neon. The sensuous female curve of the water over the gigantic horseshoe-shaped cliff. The Niagara Ball suspended in the air choked with mist and the smell of desire and the ghost of Annie Edson Taylor in her barrel. Sink or swim, you've got to sink or swim, spell Annie's bones. Roses always smell best when they're dying. The petals shoved into Hannelore's, Clotilde's and Friedl's hands, blooms grafted onto their fingers. The water slips over the edge of the cliff and keeps slipping. It mesmerizes, it makes Hannelore think of her old lover Hamish, think of her husband Heinrich, think of her hands on herself. The water makes Hanne wet between the between.

Annie picked out every stick of lumber herself, making sure that each piece was perfect—sturdy staves of Kentucky oak, each one an inch and a half thick and oiled individually to shed water. When it was finished, the barrel stood four and a half feet high, the staves secured by ten two-inch iron hoops, bolted to the barrel at four-inch intervals. It weighed 160 pounds.

—PIERRE BERTON, Niagara: A History of the Falls

The Royal Auditorium, 1996

Hannelore's feet in black leather shoes. The purple carpet. Black leather against purple background. They go well with the auditorium carpet. Management specifically said black shoes, and ten years ago, when she heard she got the job as a bartender-usher in the Royal Auditorium, Hannelore went out and bought herself the most comfortable black shoes she could find.

Oh Oma, you're fashionable now, squeaked Cleopatra Maria.

This was how people, especially young people, talked to women they believed were old, like the old women were freshly scrubbed puppies with big bows on their heads. The shoes were not fashionable. They were just new. People over twenty weren't supposed to own new things? Hannelore did not buy them to be *fashionable*. She bought them because Management ordered her to.

The shoes showed off the thickness in her ankles, thick ripples of skin, yes they made her feet look like canoe paddles, but they were the most comfortable brand of shoes in Kanada, the girl in the store wouldn't lie, she didn't look like the type of young woman who could lie. Very helpful she was, with long blonde hair twisted back in a bun, practising her German on Hannelore.

The clerk asked Cleopatra Maria was she adopted? Cleopatra Maria said *no*. The clerk smiled serenely at Hannelore. Hannelore busily tied then retied her shoelaces. Cleopatra Maria dropped a platform shoe very loudly.

Cleopatra Maria sulked, and Hannelore expected better because Cleopatra Maria was about to enter university, a child prodigy. Cleopatra Maria muttered something that sounded like "Fucking Aryans" but Hannelore ignored her. Hannelore's Cleopatra Maria wouldn't have said such a thing, although Hannelore's Cleopatra

Maria certainly changed personalities depending on where she was. Hannelore's Cleopatra Maria wouldn't know a word like Aryan.

Hannelore tried on the shoes in the store and wanted to disown her long, fat feet, but no matter how they looked, her feet smiled at her through the leather of the shoes. Like the house shoes she left on an airplane to Kanada so many years ago. She never thought she would find shoes like those shoes again but she did, and here they were on her wrinkly, flippery feet. Not that Hannelore ever ended up standing for four hours at a time, she and the other ushers in the Royal figured out short cuts. The only times she stood on her feet for four hours was during the annual Black and White ball. But those parties only happened once a year and she and the other ushers made a lot of money from them because the shifts were ten instead of four hours long. The busiest night of the year, when people shoved tips at the ushers even though tipping was not allowed in the Royal because it was a government-run theatre. Hannelore would try to give the tips back, call loudly to the patrons: This is a government-run institution! but it never worked and she would stand frowning with the loonie or five-dollar bill in her hand. This year she would work the Black and White ball. Tips troubled her, but not really. As long as Management didn't find out.

Dot, one of the other ushers, wore black sandals because of the foot operation she had last year and Hannelore looked doubtfully at them, the sandals did not go with the rest of the uniform, the smart bow tie and trim bolero jacket a ruined effect. Dot should have worn closed-toed shoes but her feet wouldn't allow that. She wore too many bad shoes for too many bad years as a bank teller, they destroyed her feet. At the age of seventy-one now, Dot had misshapen stumps instead of feet.

Hannelore did not approve of the sandals, they made her eyes hurt. But so did the lumpy, stinking stumps that were Dot's feet. The odour rising in the dark like damp rubber gloves under the sink too long. Toes and mildew.

Hannelore's feet on the carpet, a new carpet, the entire theatre, the lobby laid with new carpet, purple with tiny red triangles. Hannelore couldn't remember what the old carpet looked like even though she'd worked here for ten years, so she asked Dot what the old carpet looked like, Dot was here for twenty-five.

I can't remember, said Dot. But I know I liked the old one better.

So did I, said Hannelore.

What happened to the old carpet? Maybe Hannelore should have some of that old carpet for her house. In the basement.

But the new carpet was clean and plush although not as fine-looking, not like the old, faded and worn in parts, especially in front of the doors to the theatre where the patrons lined up to enter. Hannelore took their tickets three nights a week (except during Black and White balls, except during Good Friday services, except during Kiwanis festivals) and ripped the tickets along the perforated middles. Tonight *Niagara! The Musical*—the main floor tickets were the most expensive of all, sixty- and eighty-dollar tickets. Hannelore in her bifocals took the tickets, Dot in her trifocals handed out programmes and seated people, Dot waved her hands around like a stewardess on an airplane, left centre fourth row from the front Sir, said Dot. Three sections over on the other side of the theatre, in the aisle, Miss. Hannelore quick with ripping the tickets, ten years quick. Dot twenty-five years quick with the programmes. Management said that the ushers were supposed to lead people to their seats and Dot used to do this, she wished she could still do this but how—with her feet?

Holy smokes, I gave the theatre my feet, said Dot. They got 'em in a metal box in the tunnels with the extra lighting equipment!

Tonight *Niagara! The Musical.* Last month *Phantom of the Opera* showed for the last time ever like it did every four years or so. Hannelore loved Niagara Falls. Had been to visit them twice. Tonight, since it was a very good show, an inspiring show, Hannelore and Dot would pull up the chairs from the wheelchair area to make room for the wheelchairs and sit at the back of the theatre to watch the show. Management would pay them ten dollars an hour to watch, Hannelore and Dot would not pay eighty dollars, sixty dollars, they would not pay a cent for their ground floor, eighty dollar, perfect seats. Dot would slide off her black sandals for a moment in the dark, Hannelore would unbutton the first button of her blouse under the bow tie. Both women had their flashlights in their pockets. Hannelore's skin would shiver at the dry ice, the beautiful singing, always dry ice and grand choruses in the big shows, the ushers would be deeply disappointed if no dry ice appeared to set off the fire alarms at least one night during the three-month run of the show.

Tonight's musical was in town for seven months. It was the musical story of Annie Edson Taylor, the first woman to go over Niagara Falls in a barrel and live, and out of all the musicals Hannelore had seen while working at the Royal, this was the best of all. Partly because it had a happy ending, partly because the star of the show was the singing superstar Sharon-Lee Silver from New York who reminded Hannelore of her other favourite Schlager-sängerin from the fifties, Caterina Valente. (Bonnie, who worked the second floor, said Sharon-Lee Silver wasn't from New York at all and her real name was Ingeborg Kavorkian. She came from Stettler, Alberta. Bonnie was also from Stettler and knew Sharon-Lee's family from way back. Hannelore didn't believe this story. This was just Bonnie trying to grab attention for herself.) The musical was also Hannelore's favourite show because it was about Niagara Falls, and she appreciated the backdrops which were almost like the real thing, only dry. Sharon-Lee Silver sang so beautifully her voice was like a glorious noose around Hannelore's throat.

Hannelore was just happy that for once there was a musical that ended happily, not like *Les Misérables*, not like *Phantom of the Opera*, not like *Jesus Christ Superstar* and not like *Evita*. And not stupidly happy like *The Sound of Music*. *The Sound of Music* irritated Hannelore like hairs floating in her soup. For some reason the other ushers expected *The Sound of Music* to be Hannelore's favourite musical.

Edelweiss is a weed, not a song, Hannelore would say crisply.

Hannelore once walked past Sharon-Lee Silver's dressing room on her way to the main theatre to peek at the star—as long as Hannelore wore her usher's uniform she could go almost anywhere in the building—but Sharon-Lee Silver was absent. No one was in the dressing room except for a lumpy-looking grey-haired woman mending costumes and humming to herself.

Hannelore and Dot sat in their expensive seats and couldn't move their eyes from the stage.

Au revoir, Annie Edson Taylor sang—"Au Revoir" was the most famous song from the show—Au revoir, Sharon-Lee Silver sang, I'll not say good-bye because I'm coming baaack!

The world-famous actress Sharon-Lee Silver knelt in simulated Niagara River water, dry ice swirling around her, her lips red and luxurious, the curls of her blonde wig piled on her head like hairy whipped cream.

I should have worn my haaat, sang Sharon-Lee Silver, and she gave a little Can-Can kick.

Hannelore could imagine the scene: Already Anna Taylor's hair had started to come loose from its bun and splayed, cobweb across her face. She should have worn the large, feathered hat. Useless, of course, but it would have supported her, kept her head on straight. It made sense to Hannelore that a hat would have helped. Like getting hair done at the hairdresser's, purely cosmetic, but so important for the confidence.

Hannelore tried to imagine herself about to get into the barrel. She remembered Niagara Falls, how beautiful and gigantic they were, the screaming of the water. She wanted to visit them again. She would get Clotilde to go with her again.

The cushions in Annie's barrel were wet and their stuffing

deflated. Sharon-Lee Silver sang about her hands and feet, how cold they were, she fluttered her hands in the air, did a pirouette on the tips of her toes when she talked about her feet. So cold, they feel electric, sang Sharon-Lee and she tiptoed in a charming figure eight, So cold they feel ee-lec-tric! Sharon-Lee stamped and the music suddenly stopped. Cold from the water, the horror, the excitement that swallowed her whole, a rat head first down the elastic gullet of a snake. The first human to go over Niagara Falls and survive. Or the one thousand and first suicide. Dead in the coffin she designed herself.

The programme said that Anna Edson Taylor survived one Chattanooga flood, the 1886 Charleston earthquake, one fire, several armed robberies, and was married once.

Surely she'll survive one lil' ol' waterfall, chanted the chorus. And in the meantime have a ball!

Au revoir, Sharon-Lee Silver sang in a very high voice like a chickadee's, Au revoir, she whispered low like a hippo, Au revoir au revoir aurevoiraurevoirauREVOIR, she belted into the stuffy air of the auditorium, her voice soaking into the lush red velvet curtains, the red plush seats filled with fans. Her hands pouring through the air, and with her delicate, pointy toes, Sharon-Lee Silver surrendered herself to the choreographed spill of dry ice, the theatre blackout, the giant crash of cymbals and tympanies.

The audience in their eighty-dollar seats, the students holding binoculars in their nose-bleed balcony seats, forgot to clap, she was so beautiful, her performance so stunning, they sighed loud and long instead, wiped away their tears, then waited for the ushers in their matching bow ties to open the doors to the lobby and the badly run Auditorium cash bar stacked ready with intermission drinks.

Hannelore sighed. Patted her hair and straightened her bow tie. She loved this job.

Hannelore had her own adventure stories to tell, none so exciting as going over Niagara Falls in a barrel, but ones she could certainly put on a résumé.

Once a man in Hannelore's section had a heart attack right in the middle of *Les Misérables*. Management had said, No Opening The Doors During The Blackouts. But Hannelore nobly risked her job and opened and closed doors all that night, for the first time in her life Hannelore dialled 911 and administered CPR, the man's face like wax, like her father's when he died. Turned out it was only indigestion, too much Kentucky Fried Chicken, but still.

Once she ordered a man in a tuxedo and black, shiny cowboy boots to go back out the way he came because his breath smelled so badly of booze.

Do you know who that was? said Dot.

No.

Railroad Ronnie, the famous country singer.

I don't care if he was my favourite Schlagersänger Freddy singing in a sailor suit, he's not going into the theatre like that. Hannelore breathed hard and her hands shook. She hated reprimanding patrons. And she would rather watch the show from her eighty dollar seat than play policewoman.

What a theatre!

But mostly the patrons filed past, waited for their tickets to be ripped and one of the ushers would lead the patrons down the aisles to their assigned red plush seats. Even Ida, ninety-one years old next month and the longest-working usher at the Royal, lead patrons to their seats, the wrong seats and very very slowly, but still to seats. Ida was also Jewish, Hannelore couldn't help not being aware of Jewish people. Ida in her Auditorium-issued bolero jacket had been working there fifty years since the Auditorium first opened, the papers took her picture and wrote a blurb about her last month.

Dot used to crochet during the shows they didn't watch. Seen-too-many-times or bad shows. Or Hannelore and Dot would talk in the lobby. Conversations Hannelore could understand. Dot would crochet and talk while Hannelore sat and listened. Dot and her husband's forty-fifth wedding anniversary and their trip to Las Vegas, Dot's daughter Elaine who lived in Taber with a husband who hit her every time he drank.

Dot sighed, She's done what I did. Found the first man who hated her guts and married him.

Hannelore shook her head and talked about her son, and his grumpy and, Hannelore hated to say it, selfish yes selfish, wife Rosario. A good painter, but temperamental and selfish. Like most artists.

I would trade your daughter-in-law for my son-in-law in a second, said Dot.

Hannelore would protest, but tonight there was no need for lobby-talk to kill time because this was an elaborate show, the most elaborate of all, the lit-up miniature Niagara Falls set up in the lobby with tiny barrels bobbling in the water. Beside the tiny set up, a wax life-size figure of Annie Taylor, quite attractive, looking like one of Cleopatra Maria's old Barbie Dolls, standing in her barrel, on loan from the Niagara Falls Museum in Ontario.

Tonight Hannelore also knew the show's lighting man was under the stage, in the tunnels, waiting for her to walk by so he could tip his baseball cap at her like he had every night since *Niagara!* came to town. The first night she walked smartly past him through the tunnel and Ida said, He just tipped his hat at you Hannah.

And Hannelore said, What?

Her hand fled to her hair white and wavy in its pins.

Hamish the lighting man tipped his hat at Hannah, hooted Ida, and the other usher-bartenders tittered.

I seen him do that two nights ago, said Bonnie. And Hannah walked on by like she didn't even see him.

I didn't see him, said Hannelore.

The next night Hannelore hurried past Hamish the lighting

man, tried not to look at him, tried not to see him lift his hand to his cap, but she caught it, she caught the lift, she couldn't miss the tip.

But he's wearing a kilt! exclaimed Hannelore. He's a grown man in a skirt!

That's Hamish, said Dot. He's the lighting man on all the big shows. And Dot folded the afghan she was crocheting into her bag. He likes you, she said. I guess this means maybe there's sex after seventy. Not for me, I'm afraid, Dot added sadly.

That's *ridiculous*, said Hannelore. But the next night she answered his tip with a nod, a curt out-of-my-way nod, and she could feel her heart pump through the fabric of her beige, special occasion coat.

Hannelore thought about him so much she forgot to talk when people talked to her. Dot would stare into Hannelore's face and say, What planet are you on? and only then would Hannelore remember to talk. Hannelore thought about Hamish's not talking too. Didn't know what she thought. Heinrich killed in 1940, she thought. And Hannelore left a widow with a small baby. But Heinrich used to talk a lot.

Men.

Hannelore didn't care if the other ushers knew that Hamish watched her, told Management, made Hannelore lose her job, Hannelore was too old to care, seventy-five next month, and she'd been working here at the Royal Auditorium for ten years now, not once late, always volunteering for extra shifts.

And who was this Hamish anyway? Some show-business person. Flaky, Rosario called show-business people. Hannelore would wear her uniform with the same pride she always had, nothing to be ashamed of. Nothing. She would ignore how red her face got, and how her heart beat so hard when she thought about him she became afraid for her blood pressure.

Hamish the lighting man. His filthy green kilt and brown cigar teeth. He started smiling at her and she could tell he smoked cigars.

Or drank tea like English people. Or maybe malnutrition from the war, her teeth were bad from the war, she had to wear a dental plate because of the war and she worried about her real teeth. Whoever heard of a lighting man in a kilt? The eternal baseball cap. Hannelore's husband was perfectly kempt when he was alive. Even first thing in the morning. His hair combed, naturally combed, and slick, his clothes clean and pressed. Even his pyjamas kept their smooth ironed lines. Kempt.

The tunnels under the stage where the ushers passed through on their way to and from the main theatre. The biggest theatre in Western Canada, the most modern, the tunnels left over from before the renovations, a leftover from an uglier, tackier past. They reminded Hannelore of air-raid shelters and for this reason they made her nervous when she walked through them alone, but they also reminded her of the hot colour of her coffee in the morning heating her throat and firing her blood, like being under water. The tunnels were like wading through pure adrenaline now that Hamish tipped his cap at her every night.

Watch out for the tunnels, warned Management. Nothing has ever happened there, but ushers should not walk through unaccompanied.

At the end of each shift, Hannelore and the other ushers walked through the tunnels, some arm-in-arm, so tired they wanted to drop straight to the cold concrete floor and never get back up. Their shoes echoed through the tunnels and they talked and laughed loudly, sighed loudly, banged the doors loudly to scare off the ghosts, the humans.

Got the flu shot, eh, said Marlene.

Did it hurt? asked Bonnie.

No no.

Cuz I know some people got the shot and their arms hurt for days, said Bonnie.

Doesn't cure it but prevents it.

Doesn't cure it but prevents it, said Ida.

But it prevents it, said Ruth.

Their voices bounced off the concrete walls and fell at their feet.

Saw a mouse! said Gertrude. Yuck!

Just a mouse.

Need traps down here, said Estelle.

By then the ushers had reached the other end of the tunnels and they stepped out above ground into the night.

They were all at least sixty years old—young people never lasted as usher-bartenders at the Royal. Many of the older women knew ghosts on a coffee and cookies, scotch and water basis. Kept galleries of ghosts on their walls among photos of family. Ghosts as old as the hat on Ida's head.

I don't care about fashion, said Ida. S'long's my noodle's warm.

And the other ushers laughed, Ida their pet, the one they had to look out for.

Marlene drove home to Vince, Marian to her son Peter and husband Lance, Estelle to Frank. Gertrude went home to her empty house. Her husband dead these five years. To the wall of pictures and endless cups of tea with the television set and waiting for her daughter-in-law to call her. Her son always too busy to talk. Ida's daughter picked her up and tucked her in bed after the long shifts like Ida was one and not ninety-one. Her daughter Sarah told her she didn't have to work anymore but Ida couldn't forget the year Sarah lost her engineering job and Ida supported them both on her usher job. I will die tearing tickets, Ida said.

Marjory took the bus to her bachelor apartment which she could barely afford. She ushered at the Royal and also Commercial Theatre downtown for six dollars an hour. During the day she cleaned houses. Cleaning's not so bad, she said. You're mostly alone. She was trying to save up for a trip to Florida with her sister next year.

Bonnie took the train to her empty house, but to *her* house; she

75

got to keep it after the divorce, people kept telling her to get a guard dog for protection and company, but she'd been cleaning up her husband's shit for fifty years before he left her, why did she want a dog? Ruth went home to her ancient mother and spent the rest of the night screening phone calls from her daughters asking her to come babysit for free. Dot kept on walking down the hill with her bad, bank-teller's feet, her husband's eyesight too bad for driving but he never picked her up when his eyes were good anyway. And she couldn't use the car except when he was in it. He said her driving was unsafe.

It's because he's German, said Dot when Hannelore wasn't around. My dad said to me, he said, Dotty I don't mind you marrying a salesman, but did he have to be a German?

The other ushers worried about Dot slipping and breaking a hip, she broke a hip last year and was laid up forever. Dot now so terrified of ice she didn't even add it to her pop, could not afford another broken hip.

Hannelore would also take the train, the deep rumble of Hannelore's thickly accented English slicing through the stream of Bonnie's high-voiced squeaks and whistles, until Bonnie got off at her stop. Hannelore would stay on the train until she got to the station by her house, and she would walk along the busy street under the trees. Shoes in summer, boots in winter. Home to her sister Clotilde, watching television with the sound cranked up so loud the windows shook. Maybe Frau Schnadelhuber would be visiting with Clotilde and stay the night, she did that sometimes when there was too much Schnapps. Frau Schnadelhuber smoking pack after pack of Camels or Winstons while she and Clotilde talked, their conversations always stopping the second Hannelore entered the room. Their hands clutched together. Hannelore couldn't stand this, the two of them and their perverted conversations. The silent sitting-room blanketed in a cigarette haze that rubbed Hannelore's eyes like sandpaper. Hannelore didn't approve of Frau Schnadelhuber, although

Hannelore would never have found her usher job without Frau Schnadelhuber's help.

Even without the ushers the tunnels were busy. Stored lighting equipment, extra chairs, spiders and mice. Extra props from the current show, actors or technicians muffling the sounds of their secret sexual intercourse. The tunnels sizzled with darkness.

The Royal Auditorium. The biggest, most important theatre west of Manitoba.

In order to elude the police, who were making a half-hearted attempt to stop what the authorities regarded as a potential suicide, Russell had decided that Annie should push off from Grass Island in midstream a mile and a half above the cataract. There she was photographed with her barrel, and there, at her request, the members of her entourage and the press retreated to the far side of the island while she, hidden in the reeds, modestly peeled off hat, jacket and outer skirt. Then, attired in a short black skirt, blue-and-white shirtwaist, black stockings and tan slippers, she pronounced herself ready for the ordeal.

—PIERRE BERTON, Niagara: A History of the Falls

Niagara Falls, Canada: Thursday, October 24, 1996: 6:08 A.M.

Yes, maybe Hannelore should have worn her uniform, she wonders if they will make it in the newspapers back in Germany. Maybe the women at the Royal would see her picture in the paper. She should have worn her uniform, then people who didn't know her would be able to identify her body. She could have worn her name-tag.

Frau Taylor wore her hat to the take-off, refused to change from her long skirt into her short skirt before she was actually at the vessel because anything other than a long skirt in town

Clotilde wonders what in the hell she was thinking. This was exactly what their mother had told her specifically not to do, let Hannelore go crazy with her dangerous ideas.

She peers in the filtered, watery light at Hannelore, her face dark under the helmet, impossible to tell what she is thinking also all the lurching around, have they even gone over, she remembers feeling her stomach come up through her mouth, but that happened several times, they could have gone over a hundred waterfalls and Clotilde would never be able to tell

Frau Schnadelhuber remembers the time after the war when there were all those bombs fallen into the ground around Oranienberg. She and the other surviving Resistance members who worked for the General's Wife took a crash course in bomb defusal. And at first it was frightening. Klüsener blown up during a routine defusal right in front of her. The hairs on her forearms and the back of her neck still stand up when she hears a particular whine of airplane engine, that tinny scream that means a bomb is about to turn would not have been appropriate. What was Hannelore thinking? A jaunty, fuck 'em all farewell would have been so much better in her uniform. And a photo before they got in the vessel! What were they thinking, they forgot the camera, she can see the camera in the bottom of her suitcase full of film.

Hannelore is surprised at the woman's face suddenly in the window. The woman with the slash in her forehead and the large feathered hat? Hannelore smiles at the face through the fortified plexi-glass window, the face grim and water-bloated. The queen of the mist of course.

the difference. Her blood rushing and bubbling, her heart hasn't had this much exercise in years. All right, so a glass of Sekt first thing in the morning is not the smartest way to begin a holiday in Niagara Falls.

another street into rubble and massacre more of her neighbours. She lived through the bombs, became an expert with the pliers and the wire clippers until she got pregnant, met Karl, a Canadian soldier, and got married. He was the best-looking man she had ever met. His eyelashes were a little too long for a man's she remembers. Eventually he said he wanted to move back to Canada. She didn't realize what she was giving up. Oh well. At least she has her hat. She will come out in style.

Frau Schnadelhuber's hands at her sides feel that her skirt is missing, nothing but her nyloned legs. She runs her hands up

and down her
thighs and the skirt
is definitely gone.
Somehow her skirt
has vaporized. Just
like a bomb hit it at
ground zero. Frau
Schnadelhuber is
sure they must be
floating upside
down. She sees her
face reflected in the
window. Strange
angles and optics
can do magic things
with the eyes.

The Niagara Ball, suspended between descent and ascent under the water at the bottom of the Falls, parks for a moment beside the mud-coated, water-bloated corpse of Annie Edson Taylor, fully dressed and furious. Annie Edson Taylor shakes her polluted, fish-chewed fist at the round window of the vessel and when she speaks her bloated toad's mouth ejects giant bubbles, silver and poisonous as mercury.

Get the hell outta my water, she says. *I was here first and I'm gonna be here last.*

Americans! says Hannelore in exasperation.

Americans, says Clotilde. She remembers how when the Americans arrived a lot of people waved from the windows and the great wave of amnesia descended forever. Neighbours who supported Hitler and the Party suddenly waving from the windows and welcoming the Americans like their own sons. Personal histories changed, allegiances erased, everyone a resister. The Americans with their silent, rubber-soled boots. Like cats through the streets.

My daughter is half American. Don't you slag Americans, says Frau Schnadelhuber. Now you! she shouts to the window fogged with their breath and sweat, You fuck off! You're blocking our view!

Edmonton, Canada, 1985

A year after she and Clotilde moved to Kanada, Hannelore agreed to move with the family to their new house, on the other side of town, almost an hour's drive away.

Clotilde and I would be happy to go, Hannelore said. You'll make sure the house fits all of us?

Mutti, said Dieter. He shook his head slowly.

I'll run and tell Clotilde, said Hannelore.

You should leave them alone, said Clotilde from behind her book. They are still young, they need their room. You always want to be in other people's rooms. I don't want to move. If you make me move I'll check myself into a home.

You shouldn't read in the dark, said Hannelore.

Cleopatra Maria was painting Clotilde's toenails purple. Cleopatra Maria a child of few words, more interested in setting fires with her magnifying glass in the big blue garbage bin with the other strange suburban children than playing with her toys. The suburbs. Cleopatra Maria was a product of the Kanadian suburbs and maybe this was why she was so out of place anywhere else. Hannelore remembered the howls of the coyotes who lived at the edge of the suburbs at night and she held Cleopatra Maria close to her. Cleopatra Maria carried off by coyotes.

Clotilde's nails hooked like claws, and large—perfect for painting. Clotilde began to yell her spontaneous yell, the yell that blew open doors and windows and joggled her feet so much, she knocked over the open bottle of polish and Cleopatra Maria began to scream like when she was a baby. Clotilde screamed too: I already moved once from Germany to come to this frozen hell, said Clotilde. Now I'm not going to move again! I am too old to move, I won't move one centimetre! Don't interfere!

Clotilde dropped her book, and Hannelore rushed over to pick it up.

Don't interfere! shouted Cleopatra Maria in her disturbingly perfect German with her eyes just like Hannelore's mother's.

Hannelore crumpled up newspapers and stuffed them in the bottom of boxes she took from the alley behind the Safeway. She chose the cleanest, sturdiest boxes, brushed off the dirt with a cloth she brought especially in a plastic Safeway bag. Layers of identically sized newspaper, the china cups and saucers wrapped up separately. Furniture tape to seal up the boxes. "FRAGIL" Hannelore wrote on the boxes. She bent from the waist as she worked, to save her knees.

We left Germany because of you, said Rosario from the doorway. Rosario stepped between the boxes of crushed newspaper, she slipped on a green photo album.

Don't interfere between me and my son, said Hannelore.

You drive us crazy, said Rosario. You drive us up the wall, don't you understand? We need to live by ourselves. You and your son, she said contemptuously. Don't interfere between me and my husband.

Downstairs, Dieter turned the music on the headphones up louder. He sprinkled sugar in the yeast and warm water, stirred, and set the bowl to the side.

Up the wall? thought Hannelore. Up the wall? What a strange expression, what is she? a fly? Hannelore didn't let Rosario's words push her from her fine spot in the sun, she put three photo albums into a cardboard box that used to hold oranges, Hannelore was a dachshund stretched out in the sun and she would not be budged, not by any kicks or prods or patent leather high heels. Rosario's strange foreign smell, acidic, corrosive, her skinny flailing body under a turtleneck that was too tight and showed the droop of her tiny breasts, a skirt that was far too short, a tiny strip of leather barely covering her crotch. Her pouty forty-year-old belly above birdy stick-legs.

Rosario was afraid of age, she clung to bright colours and young styles even though she was thirty-seven. Almost forty. This would give her grief. Hannelore had no trouble assimilating, old age would not hook into her with its claws. A woman of forty in a leather miniskirt. Rosario dyed her hair, obvious from the grey strands that appeared then disappeared like shooting stars. Rosario wore leather and suede jackets with shoulder pads and matching miniskirts. High-heeled, pointy-toed shoes with imitation zippers up the backs just like a prostitute's, and sheer stockings that emphasized her bony ankles and knobbly knees. That smell, corrosive. Old chemical sweat, sweat with a hint of grape juice, garlic and floor cleaner.

You can't live with us, said Rosario. You can't. You'll just have to find another place. The new place won't fit you. It's only big enough for three people. Dieter, Cleopatra Maria, and me!

Rosario's voice shrill like a blender's.

Rosario cried, her mouth turned down like a clown's and oily tears wet her face. The first time Rosario had ever shown tears to Hannelore. Hannelore felt like a monster. Glad about her daughter-in-law's tears because they meant she won, but still a monster.

No crying, said Hannelore huskily, crying always contagious. No crying now.

Hannelore could not handle the unbearable heat that went into her head when she was about to cry.

Hannelore rested her hands on one of Rosario's shoulder-pads, the squish of the soft, pliant leather and foam.

Now look what you did, said Clotilde, glasses sliding down her nose, newspaper crunched in her hand. Look what you did. I told you, I told you, young people need their privacy I told you not to meddle, I told you I told you I told you. Meddling in people's lives, interrupting their lives.

You shut your mouth, said Hannelore, You shut your big fat chimpanzee mouth.

That's it, said Clotilde. This time I'm not coming back, I'm checking myself into Silver Glade. I didn't want to come here, you made me come here. I'm leaving.

You came here of your own free will! said Hannelore.

What's going on? asked Rosario, her face wet, her nose snotty and damp. These old people and their theatre, thought Rosario.

Later Clotilde helped Hannelore take the albums and china back out of the boxes. Hannelore would stay in the townhouse for now while she looked for somewhere else to live. Decorate it decently. Enough of Rosario's bead-curtains and Jew art. Not Jew art, Hannelore didn't mean Jew art, the art had nothing to do with Jews, just paintings with unnecessarily naked people, this is what she meant. She clapped her hand to her mouth even though she'd said nothing, nothing out loud about the Jew art. Clotilde slowly wiped down the shiny albums with a dust cloth and stacked them back on the shelf. Rosario put the boxes back in her studio. Hannelore's eyes were hot and red like boiled eggs, her heart soggy and deflated.

For dinner they ate pizza with pepperoni. So much cheese. So much cholesterol, but luckily she and Clotilde had their cholesterol and blood pressure pills. Clotilde would ask Hannelore later to help her find her travel toiletries. Clotilde's new home Silver Glade.

Hannelore and Rosario sat silent at opposite sides of the dinner table until Dieter and Cleopatra Maria cleared away the plates. To calm herself, Rosario went to her little room and began making a tapestry of the pizza. She sifted through bundles of pizza-coloured yarn, began playing with sketches of the pizza.

Would you like something to drink? asked Hannelore from the door.

That would be nice, said Rosario, not looking up.

Juice? Tea?

A glass of white wine, said Rosario.

Hannelore violently opened a fresh bottle of white wine and poured the wine into a glass. Then into another glass for herself. She put the glasses on a tray and took the tray to Rosario's workroom.

They drank the wine without talking, no sound but hot air blasting through the heat vents.

Hannelore looked at the sausages in the glass case neatly lined up, sliced at identical angles. Her feet had led her to the delicatessen. Her hands had put her beige coat on her body and her beige shoes on her feet and she walked out the door. Nothing in the house. She wanted to find a cliff to think about throwing herself over, wouldn't her son miss her then. Wouldn't he regret leaving her then in a strange country, a different language, his old mother.

The sausages, the pans of boiled red cabbage, chicken Schnitzel, firm cheesecake, and Bienenstiche in the dessert case. Red cabbage, she always loved red cabbage. . . .

My son is going to leave me, blurted Hannelore to the waitresses and cooks, not any single woman, just all of them in their Dirndl dresses and puffy bosoms, to the sausages in their case, to the cabbage steaming in its pan. Her eyes and her mouth watered.

He is abandoning me and I will be alone.

Hannelore started to cry, first the burning of the eyes, the hot water boiling them red, then the spill. The water spilled from the rims of her eyes and the spilling was always the worst for Hannelore, the most embarrassing moment, the point of no return when the spill happened. Tears splattered onto her glasses and Hannelore scrubbed at her eyes with the handkerchief one of the waitresses stuffed in her hand. Hannelore sat behind the counter, behind the row of deep metal pans overflowing with food, the Sauerkraut, the warm, only lightly spiced potato salad, the slabs of fried and breaded Schnitzel. The smells made her bawl into the Bavarian handkerchief because once again she would be alone and Clotilde had lost her marbles and was trying to check herself into a home and what was she supposed to do with a lost-her-marbles Clotilde? How could Hannelore care for Clotilde and her stubbornness? Every time Clotilde cooked there were potatoes or beans or cabbage like charcoal tumours forgotten in the pot. Hannelore would be sixty-five in January.

Jesus Christ you need to get out of the house. Sounds like you need a job, said one of the women in her Dirndl dress, Frau Schnadelhuber. I know how it feels. Children. My daughter only calls me when she wants free marriage counselling.

You want me to work here? asked Hannelore. One of the scorched potatoes fell off the side of the pot that was her heart.

Hannelore looked around at the metal pots full of German-style minestrone and Perogies, the glass refrigerator and microwave oven.

Here? Hannelore repeated.

Of course not, scoffed Frau Schnadelhuber. You're from the North, you don't know what good food is, o.k.?

Hannelore let out a damp and windy sob.

I have a friend who's an usher at the Royal Auditorium.

An usher? I don't know how to usher. I'm too old to get a job now, who would want to hire me? I have never worked outside of my house. I've never had a job. My sister is the one who worked. My father said Clotilde could work and that I—

The Royal? Hannelore thought, The theatre? Dieter had taken Hannelore to see *Die Fledermaus* there.

It doesn't matter, said Frau Schnadelhuber. They like old house-wives they can underpay and exploit. My friend loves it. Gets her away from her bastard of a husband one or two nights a week. You apply for a job, o.k.? I'll tell her to look out for your name.

The "r" in Frau Schnadelhuber's pronunciation of "job" trilled with a Bavarian trill, the ecstatic trill of a robin pulling a seven-foot-long worm from the earth.

You will get a job and you'll be so busy you won't have time to think about your ingrate son. Now stop crying.

Frau Schnadelhuber pulled out a piece of paper and in between forking out rubbery slabs of Schnitzel, rolling Bratwurst onto plates, and during Frau Schnadelhuber's break when she smoked half a pack of Lucky Strikes, she and Hannelore composed the Résumé.

What is your name? asked Hannelore and the ash from the tip of Frau Schnadelhuber's cigarette dropped like a dead butterfly.

Hey Frau Schnadelhuber! shouted one of the cooks, "Oma Hupfel" said her tag. You slacking off again? and she started to laugh outrageously. You just watch your purse! shouted Oma Hupfel through the open doorway to Hannelore, Our Frau Schnadelhuber likes to steal things!

You shut up Hupfel! shouted Frau Schnadelhuber, her cigarette quivering.

Oma Hupfel went back to slicing the blood-sausage on the machine with firm even strokes, still chuckling, her large arms like meat stroking the sausage, her puffy bosom in its Los Angeles version of a Dirndl crowding her double chin.

You don't listen to her, said Frau Schnadelhuber to Hannelore. She's full of shit. Now sign the letter "Yours truly" in English.

So Frau Schnadelhuber stole things sometimes. So what. As if Hupfel's record was so clean. It's not like Frau Schnadelhuber stole cars or houses. Once she stole a sofa, another time a forty-pound wheel of cheese from a grocery store, but these were not major items. She never stole other people's purses—that was pure Hupfel *Quatsch*.

Frau Schnadelhuber watched Hannelore drink coffee and try to scribble her entire life onto a single sheet of paper.

Stealing just a leftover habit from the war when there was almost nothing to steal and from living with her asshole of a husband Karl. The old days before the delicatessen when she had no job, no money, only Karl to give her money for the baby, but that was all he would give her and he decided exactly how much she needed for baby food, milk, baby clothes. He would make her bring him the worn-out, out-grown clothes, bring them to him while he inspected them to make sure she wasn't lying. She never *wasted* and that was the most humiliating, that he thought she was *wasteful*. She knew want, so she stole. Stealing wasn't that hard if you had the right attitude. Once she stole seven bags of groceries. Filled her cart and walked out the door, just out the door. All in the attitude, this is what her old boss the General's Wife told her during the war: Attitude. The General's Wife and her smuggling of SS plans, very high up in the Resistance, was nothing but attitude. Frau Schnadelhuber would have died for the Wife, that was how much loyalty Frau Schnadelhuber had for the Wife, the greatest spy who ever lived. Frau Schnadelhuber worked as the Wife's chauffeur, all the men gone off to war. She would drive the Wife's black Mercedes through the streets, use her superior driving skills to outrun suspected Gestapo agents. She was the Wife's most prized employee. When Frau Schnadelhuber successfully stole another tv guide from the supermarket, she did so out of respect for the Wife and disrespect to Karl.

Now what do I put? asked Hannelore.

Sign your name, answered Frau Schnadelhuber. She threw her cigarette down and it rolled into the shopping mall parking lot.

Not that the world *owed* Frau Schnadelhuber, but the older she got, the less of the world she seemed entitled to. The less space she was allowed to take up, the more she could be ignored in line-ups. Then the job at the delicatessen. She was still invisible as a generic German behind the plates of food, but not because she was *old*— she still remained in *control*. Frau Schnadelhuber never stole from work. Her job was more her home than her home. Frau Schnadelhuber wiped her spectacles on her apron. Well the job saved her life. What else could a seventy-five-year-old, out-of-work Resistance spy's chauffeur do in a foreign country? Not much.

Good, said Frau Schnadelhuber. Now get Hupfel to type that up in the back room and then take it in. Here is the address of the Auditorium. I have to go make more potato salad. The lunch rush will be here soon and Hupfel is useless on her own.

So the family moved from the townhouse in the suburbs to a tiny apartment an hour away on the other side of town closer to Rosario's new job at the city art college. For Rosario's new job.

But won't it take longer for you to get to work, Dieter? asked Hannelore. This will put you out.

But Mutti, I won't be working there much longer. They don't want me anymore. I'm redundant don't you see, said Dieter in his English-softened German, but his voice did a fat man's pirouette, and he smiled broadly and turned around the rim of his baseball cap. He snapped on Waldmann the II's leash and sauntered happily out the door, the bend in his neck gone, his hands swinging vigorously at his sides.

You will come visit every day after work? trembled Hannelore. Won't you?

Mama, he said reproaching.

After I came to this country to be with you? One day you won't be able to visit me, even if you want to. You will look down on my cold, dead face and regret your life.

Every weekend, Dieter said.

Every weekend! blurted Rosario into her mirror, her head full of green, spiky curlers. All right, she said. You could take Cleopatra Maria with you sometimes, give me time to work in the studio.

Almost every weekend, Dieter slept on the pull-out couch, mowed the lawn, took Tante Clotilde out for cappuccino and to the newspaper store, fixed the hisses in the toilet. Watched Dr. Who at midnight Saturday night. Hannelore never understood the attraction of Dr. Who, but watched with Dieter. Cleopatra Maria cried when Rosario told her they were moving, so every second day Cleopatra Maria took the hour-long bus-ride and stayed at her Oma and Tante's house. She complained that her parents were boring and selfish, and Hannelore knew her granddaughter's perceptiveness came from her side of the family.

Mutti, you should get a dog like Waldmann, said Dieter. Dogs teach you how to love.

Just don't let me catch you kissing that dog on the lips, said Hannelore.

Clotilde leaned on her cane in the doorway of one of the nursing-home rooms and watched her future roommate try to kill herself.

What are you doing? asked Clotilde.

I am trying to kill myself, said the roommate in her chair. She leaned forward in the chair, leaned farther and farther forward.

You're going to fall, said Clotilde.

I want to bang my skull on the floor and kill myself, said the roommate.

That's not so great, said Clotilde. Do you want me to call a nurse?

No.

Clotilde looked out the window of the room at the carefully mown grass. Years ago in this kind of mood, Clotilde would have visited a spa. Taken a steam bath, then a cold shower, then soaked in warm water salty with minerals and convalescence. Her body a parched iris, light and drinking in steam. Here in this new nursing home, she remembered that in these places the only water was the water that trickled from the shower-head, or went cold in the bath-tub where she was monitored by a nurse who made her scrub between the legs like a whore.

Maybe we should walk down the hall to the television, offered Clotilde. I'll help you.

Who are you? asked the roommate rudely. I remember, you're the one who thinks this is a hotel. You have a real place to live.

Clotilde pressed the button for the nurse.

All right, said Clotilde. I'll come home with you.

Good, said Hannelore.

A British woman and a Yugoslavian called me a fraud today while I was standing at the reception desk, said Clotilde. They said I've had sugar blown up my bottom for too many years. They said I was a spoiled idiot for coming here to run away from my problems.

How rude, said Hannelore.

Yes, said Clotilde. This is a beautiful country, but I can't believe how rude the people can be.

Annie, a not unintelligent woman, even if her life had been sheltered, a non-swimmer, a plump woman, was strapped into the barrel. Cushions were tucked around her. William Holloran, a boatman, pumped air into the barrel for twenty minutes with a cycle pump. His comment: "We've given her enough gas for a week."

—Percy Rowe, Niagara Falls & Falls

So Hannelore first brought home Clotilde from the nursing home, then she brought Frau Schnadelhuber over for coffee and cherry flan and Clotilde thought, High-strung.

Frau Schnadelhuber, this is my sister Fräulein Clotilde Starfinger, said Hannelore, and the three women shook hands brusquely.

But then Clotilde noticed the smooth unmade up lids of Frau Schnadelhuber's eyes behind the tiny round spectacles, strange not to see cosmetics, the vulnerability of eyes without cosmetics. The symmetrical part in Frau Schnadelhuber's hair and Clotilde thought, Low-strung?

Clotilde decided she would try Frau Schnadelhuber out.

Hannelore, said Clotilde, You forgot the sugar.

You don't take sugar.

I'll get the sugar there, Frau Schmitt, said Frau Schnadelhuber. Where is it?

No Hannelore, you get the sugar, said Clotilde. My sister will get the sugar, Frau Schnadelhuber.

We don't *eat* sugar Clotilde. I don't understand. Sugar.

Hannelore went to the kitchen for the sugar and when she got to the kitchen, she forgot what she had gone there for. She began to straighten the cutlery drawer.

In the sitting-room, Clotilde sat forward in her chair.

Frau Schnadelhuber sat back and sighed. The women looked at each other.

So you have never been married Fräulein Starfinger? asked Frau Schnadelhuber.

Not to a man, no. Clotilde licked her lips.

What else is there to marry? A goose? asked Frau Schnadelhuber. She snorted.

People see that I am not married to a man and always hope I am

99

a widow or a virgin. You are married to a man? said Clotilde.

I am a widow.

Oh, I am so sorry.

No, don't be sorry. He's not dead.

Then how can you be a widow?

Don't be so literal Fräulein Starfinger. You don't have to have lost a husband to be a widow. He left me for another woman and now I mourn for years wasted. I mourn for myself.

Frau Schnadelhuber wished Fräulein Starfinger would offer her some more coffee.

This conversation is too serious, said Frau Schnadelhuber. Your sister showed me your garden. Lovely.

Nothing grows properly in this country, said Clotilde.

Not true, not true. Very good beef here. And apples. Canada is where the Macintosh apple comes from. You know the Macintosh apple?

Macintosh apple, said Clotilde. Crummy apple juice like water.

Frau Schnadelhuber continued: So, you just left the nursing home. I could never bear to be in such a place. Your sister is taking a long time with the sugar.

Hannelore probably forgot what she went for. You are very attractive, said Clotilde suddenly, the corners of her lips arched cunningly like her eyebrows.

What?

Frau Schnadelhuber sang out the question, the conversation going in too many absurd directions at once and now this, the most absurd direction of all, Fräulein Starfinger talking about Frau Schnadelhuber's looks like Frau Schnadelhuber was a bouncing eighteen-year-old Mädchen and ripe for the picking. Or was Frau Schnadelhuber only imagining things, getting a swelled head because someone was paying attention to her even if that someone was only a woman. Frau Schnadelhuber's head felt like a pretzel. She found nothing to say so she pretended to drink from her empty cup. The last cloudy drop of coffee on the bottom of the cup rolled around and around.

Are you thirsty? asked Clotilde. Your cup is empty. Such an attractive woman should never have such. An. Empty. Cup.

Clotilde carefully poured cherry Schnapps into a fine crystal glass. Clotilde's dark brown eyes cupped Frau Schnadelhuber's chin.

Oh Clotilde! said Hannelore bustling back into the room. You and your sugar, I had to go to the basement to get the bag to fill up the pot and now you've already started pouring the Schnapps! Why couldn't you wait until after?

Fräulein Starfinger had given Frau Schnadelhuber the sex-eyes. No one had given Frau Schnadelhuber such sex-eyes in years and Frau Schnadelhuber sat in her chair rigid like a mummy from the shock. No one had looked at her, period, in years. She had assumed invisibility was the dress she always wore, and now the shock of being looked at made her remember the days when men gave her sex-eyes all the time. There was no doubt Fräulein Starfinger had given her sex-eyes, Frau Schnadelhuber could always tell sex-eyes, she was not imagining things. But now she felt stupid, she was too old for sex-eyes, she didn't like suddenly being looked at, she felt like cross-hairs were being pointed directly at her protruding and unprotected stomach and this would all collapse into a horrible joke at her expense. She crossed her hand over her belly, tipped the cup to her lips, but the drop of coffee stayed at the bottom of the cup and clapped its hands at her. The pretzel that was her head looped another loop.

When she was young, Frau Schnadelhuber considered herself attractive, her breasts were certainly stunning. She let men look at them, sometimes even touch them, in the work camp during the war to barter for cigarettes, or chocolate. Sometimes she used them now, pulled them out and pointed them at people's shocked and horrified faces, to get off charges of shop-lifting—no one should pay that much for batteries—but her breasts were not the same as when she was young. When she was young, they were so splendid she could have made love to herself every day. She used to have a prodigious brassiere and girdle collection, the names of all the people who gave her the brassieres embroidered on the insides of the left straps, until her ex-husband Karl discovered them and made her throw them out. All of them. Then he left her for another woman. Younger, naturally, with floating orbs instead of breasts—falsies, they used to call them. Now falsies had a more scientific name: silicone implants. Very expensive falsies.

When Frau Schnadelhuber looked in the mirror, she did not see an attractive woman, only a fat one. An old one.

Thank you for the afternoon, said Frau Schnadelhuber. I must go now, I have to go to work.

That was rude, said Hannelore. Frau Schnadelhuber has a good heart but seems a little stupid.

Clotilde slowly stacked the plates and saucers and cups on the tray and clumped to the kitchen.

As a child she preferred playing games with boys to dressing up dolls. She devoured adventure stories, her brain "teeming with romance." Her marriage to David Taylor, more than a dozen years her senior, was not happy. When he died of wounds suffered in the Civil War, she was left on her own.

—PIERRE BERTON, Niagara: A History of the Falls

The Royal Auditorium, 1996

Hamish has his eye on you! said Ida. I saw the way he looked at you, that lighting man. He's a devil. We've all had a hankering after him some time, haven't we Dot?

You stop, said Dot. I'm a married woman.

Dot had it bad, said Ida, What'd you do Dot? To stop the hankering?

Got a look under his kilt, said Dot.

Hoo hoo, crowed the ushers.

Hannelore took a sip of water from the cooler so cold frost shot into her brain like a flower. She straightened her bow tie in the mirror because she didn't care what they were saying, ridiculous for a woman her age to be in a bow tie, ridiculous to care about filthy, unfounded gossip.

Hannelore combed her hair with her comb, swiftly, nonchalantly, a mistake. She never combed her hair in front of the other ushers, why did she do it now? The comb teeth were too close together, the comb tore her hair out. She wanted to wield the comb like a "shut-up" wand, but instead the comb just pulled out a big clump of her hair. She saw old age wedged between the teeth, old age was what she always pulled from her head when she tried to tidy her hair quickly, alarming coils of white hair, the growing pink of her scalp. In the mornings, or by herself in the auditorium bathroom, she picked cautiously at her scalp with her wide-toothed, tortoise-shell comb instead of inflicting the carnage of the hairbrush. The mirror showed the light shining through the cumulus of her hair, hair too fine and fragile for a much longer life. She pulled the hair from the comb, rolled it into a loose ball and put it in the inside pocket of her bolero jacket.

Clotilde's hair plentiful as crab grass, the same as when Clotilde was a young woman. Thick and grey and tough like straw, chopped off squarely, too short at the neck, pulled back unceremoniously from her face and jammed with two pins, one on either side. The no-nonsense, practical hairstyle of a lapsed communist.

Frau Schnadelhuber told her daughter Hedwig, Hedwig, she said, your mind could never fathom the bullshit in the world. Always be sure to keep your mouth shut when you know there's bullshit about to be thrown around. Frau Schnadelhuber smoked, she reached over and turned the volume on the stereo higher.

Hedwig tapped her cigarette on the side of the Hummel ashtray like the fake smoker she was.

Hedwig, said Frau Schnadelhuber. The right attitude will save you every time. Just don't let them know you know you're up to your neck in bullshit or else only one thing can happen: blackmail or death.

Is this something the General's Wife told you? said Hedwig.

Of course. And when in doubt, my girl, just flash the breasts. You have my breasts, said Frau Schnadelhuber proudly, you can go far in the world with such breasts.

Ma, I'm already in my fifties. I guess I would've gotten there by now if I was going to get anywhere. I'm just a bitter divorcée like you.

You listen to your mother, said Frau Schnadelhuber. You want another cigarette?

Hedwig tapped her cigarette again and lifted it to her mouth. She breathed in the smoke shallowly. Hedwig didn't smoke, but today she smoked. To feel closer to her mother.

Frau Schnadelhuber stared at Hedwig's fingers, the cigarette held in them awkwardly, like strips of pickled herring.

Hedwig waited.

The memory of Clotilde Starfinger's eyes on her body forced Frau Schnadelhuber to turn up the volume on the stereo. Hedwig put in her ear plugs.

Man, do I need a beer, shouted Frau Schnadelhuber. You want a beer?

The next weekend Frau Schnadelhuber sent the sisters a bouquet of thank-you flowers. Thank you for the visit.

Hannelore came in to show off her usher's uniform to Frau Schnadelhuber, and Frau Schnadelhuber nodded.

Oma Hupfel sliced meat because she liked to slice meat—slicing meat was the only thing she would do without being asked—and listened in on the conversation. Oma Hupfel lazy as the day was long.

They pay good there? asked Oma Hupfel. Maybe I should go work there too. Won't have to watch my purse all the time, she said and laughed in Frau Schnadelhuber's direction.

Hupfel, one of these days your head's going to be sitting in the refrigerator next to the apple juice, said Frau Schnadelhuber.

Oma Hupfel began to hum along to the rhythm of her hands moving the sausage on the meat cutter. She had been on local television, "Tele-Treffpunkt," a German show on cable, she was a television star. She was meant to be humoured.

So you got my flowers? said Frau Schnadelhuber.

Yes, they were very fine, said Hannelore. She didn't mention how Clotilde had fussed like a three-year-old over finding matching tablecloths to set under the bouquet in their glass vase, the fight Hannelore and Clotilde had had over Clotilde's insistence they use the best gold linen tablecloth that had belonged to their mother.

Fräulein Starfinger, your sister, she liked them too?

Yes, but she isn't one for flowers.

Oh that's too bad.

She'll go steal her a better gift, shouted Oma Hupfel from the meat cutter.

I would like you to come over to my house for some coffee and cake, said Frau Schnadelhuber. Sunday afternoon at four.

Sunday afternoon. After our swim. Yes.

Good.

Good.

Good, said Oma Hupfel.

The two of you will be there, said Frau Schnadelhuber.

Good.

Good.

Good.

The fall of meat on the other side of the cutter into Oma Hupfel's hand, like fine fabric swirling on a ballroom floor.

You're not invited Hupfel! shouted Frau Schnadelhuber.

Oma Hupfel worked the meat through the cutter, thought about all the make-up they made her wear for her television appearance eleven years ago on "Tele-Treffpunkt." She wore her best dress that day. The light green one with the pleats in the skirt.

Is your daughter adopted? asked Hannelore politely.

No, said Hedwig, coming in with the tray of sliced cake, the coffee butler full of steaming, grit-your-teeth coffee. Anything else you want Ma? Hedwig's hands on her hips.

No, said Frau Schnadelhuber. Hedwig, you go now.

Well, you call me you need anything, said Hedwig.

I'm not dead yet, said Frau Schnadelhuber.

Soon, said Hedwig, and she left the room.

Only if you kill me in my sleep! shouted Frau Schnadelhuber.

No, she is not adopted, said Frau Schnadelhuber. Her father was an American soldier. Turned out he was part African. An African in America with white skin. Did I have some explaining to do! Then I met my husband Karl.

But your daughter is a Black Woman, said Hannelore.

Hannelore don't be daft, said Clotilde. Clotilde's hair still moist at the roots from her Sunday morning swim, her hands on the table next to her plate, her eyes on Frau Schnadelhuber's sturdy hands. Very fine hands.

That is a beautiful ring Frau Schnadelhuber, said Clotilde and she sucked at her china cup full of coffee. A very elaborate china cup with filigreed edges. Obviously a best cup. The ring. Garnet.

From the war, said Frau Schnadelhuber. A gift from my old employer. She was a top spy for the Resistance. A general's wife. Very wealthy.

Hannelore jammed a slice of cake into her mouth to stop the bubbling sound of "liar" from escaping her throat. Hannelore tried to catch Clotilde's eye, but Clotilde ignored her.

Hannelore and Frau Schnadelhuber. Their mouths crammed full of cake. Frau Schnadelhuber seated at the edge of the table playing with her ring, the handle of her cup. She shifted her bottom around on the seat of the chair.

The following Monday Frau Schnadelhuber and Clotilde met in the Central Library to go for coffee and cake. Clotilde was reading a week-old newspaper from Frankfurt. Frau Schnadelhuber sat beside Clotilde, her hands in her lap, her forehead wrinkled like crepe paper.

I'm ready, said Frau Schnadelhuber.

For coffee? asked Clotilde. Good. Can you help me put on my coat?

No. Not for coffee.

Not for coffee?

For you to kiss me. I've thought about it and I would like you to kiss me.

Clotilde grasped Frau Schnadelhuber's hand in a hearty shake and kissed her on both cheeks.

Nooooooo, whispered Frau Schnadelhuber, she began to sniff.

All right, said Clotilde. But not here.

Clotilde and Frau Schnadelhuber made fumbly, first-time love in the spacious bathroom cubicle with bars along the walls designed for people in wheelchairs. Frau Schnadelhuber's glasses dipped into the toilet and Clotilde's hearing aid popped out. Frau Schnadelhuber's braids unwound from her head.

I am out of practice, apologized Frau Schnadelhuber.

Like riding a bicycle, said Clotilde. Not so easy anymore with the arthritis. But sex cures all ailments.

I never owned a bicycle, breathed Frau Schnadelhuber.

Me neither, said Clotilde. Put your bifocals on, she whispered. I like the way you look in them.

Frau Schnadelhuber giggled.

They kissed long and wetly, Frau Schnadelhuber's skirt hiked up around her roly-poly waist. The smell of toilet disinfectant, the smell of Frau Schnadelhuber, the smell of library books and newspapers.

So, you work in a delicatessen, said Clotilde.

Yes, said Frau Schnadelhuber.

Frau Schnadelhuber tried to keep her arms raised so that her breasts would look rounder and fuller, this was a trick she learned as a girl. She had beautiful breasts when she was young.

So you work in a delicatessen . . . breathed Clotilde, So you work in a delicatessen . . . so you work in a delicatessen.

Yes, said Frau Schnadelhuber, her arms slowly descending because of the warmth of Clotilde's breath, like fine cognac churning through her veins. Her arms descended because of the pleasure, because they were tired, because what her exhausted old breasts looked like didn't matter right now, because of the liquid in the hiss of "delicatessen." Frau Schnadelhuber hadn't had sex in twenty-five years after she found out her husband had venereal disease, a rotten penis, rotted through and through he was. He slept in his room, she slept fitfully in hers, and then he left her for another woman. Bastard.

I work in a delicatessen, Frau Schnadelhuber whispered.

Clotilde's body was certainly not young, no falsies, nothing false except for maybe a bit of plastic and some screws in her hip. Clotilde inhabited her own body so fully it couldn't be parcelled off into sections from other people's looking. When Clotilde kissed her, Frau Schnadelhuber felt her own spirit begin to leak into the empty, dried up parts of her body. Frau Schnadelhuber, her hands tangled in her long braids, felt hornier and happier than a city of rabbits.

Do you like books? Newspapers? asked Clotilde, Clotilde's breasts obviously no falsies, Frau Schnadelhuber's braids draped over Clotilde's shoulders.

I adore them, said Frau Schnadelhuber. I once accepted two days' worth of food in exchange for a book.

That's good, said Clotilde. It's good we met in the Library then.

Banff, Canada, 1986

Today the Banff hot springs were thirty-nine degrees Celsius, so full
of minerals Hannelore's, Clotilde's, and Frau Schnadelhuber's bodies bobbed up in the blue steaming water, they sat on the ledge and
cooled their steaming shoulders. The mountains and the giant pine
trees, the simmering water, the tourists who boiled around them,
toads in a smoking pot.

This water was quiet but there was always the danger of boiling
to death—if they boiled to death it would be a sweet death here in
the mountains among the birds and the wilderness. Bears. Many
bears in Kanada.

Very poetic, their bodies floating face-down on the surface of
the water, their eyes wide open like hard-boiled eggs. Grey and
white hairs waving tendrils, long, white hair like the Furies', the
three of them. Frau Schnadelhuber, Clotilde, Hannelore.

No, said Hannelore. She touched her lip fretfully.

Yes, said Clotilde.

Yes, said Frau Schnadelhuber.

You always do this Clotilde, fluttered Hannelore. I thought at
last you'd grown out of it.

So? said Clotilde.

Do you have to *hold hands* in front of me? In public? asked Hannelore.

The Furies' white and steel-coloured gobs of hair more power-
ful than blood pressure pills.

Hannelore was certain people probably had intercourse in this
water. There were no limits to human perversion, humans could
not help polluting, the wave of her flashlight in the Auditorium
over people twisting like worms sliced by the shovel in freshly-
turned earth and Hannelore always surprised, always disgusted,

and perhaps always just a little curious but this curiosity she didn't want to understand.

But the hot springs *seemed* clean. Frau Schnadelhuber sat with her head back, her mouth parted and eyes closed above the water. Clotilde sat on the ledge up to her neck in water, her head sliced off from the rest of her body by the liquid surface, her eyes round and shiny.

Hannelore watched their hands. Connected in the blue of the water.

"What is it?"

"The barrel is leaking," Annie said.

"How much water is there in it?"

"About a pailful."

"Well, that will not hurt you. You will be over the Falls and rescued in a few minutes and the water will help to keep you awake. We're going to cast off now. Goodbye."

"Goodbye," replied Annie faintly.

—PIERRE BERTON, Niagara: A History of the Falls

The Royal Auditorium, 1996

She's getting bored, said Bonnie.

You can tell?

She's practically yawning on stage.

Sharon-Lee Silver half-heartedly bounced her way across the stage these days and it was killing the ushers.

Sharon-Lee Silver was getting bored, and the usher-bartenders tried to root for her, tried to channel their enthusiasm and energy to the stage, but it was no good. Sharon-Lee went through the motions during the "Au Revoir" number, she fudged the words and sang "tra la la" instead of trying to remember the part. She waved her feathered hat around like it was a slice of pizza and at the end kissed her wealthy hotel owner like he was an over-ripe slab of beef.

By then of course, everyone who worked at the Royal knew the show inside out, knew all the songs, knew all the tricks.

I could do it better than her, said Marjory.

Maybe, said Marian, but who would pay to see you?

The ushers laughed.

Poor Sharon-Lee, someone said.

Yes, it's so hard being a star and having the world at your feet. All *I* get is bunions.

I still believe that Sharon-Lee is a genius, said Hannelore gravely, and I wish you would all stop making fun of her. She went to the women's washroom to get more ice from the freezer.

Sieg Heil! whispered Marjory to Hannelore's back, and Ida gave Marjory a horrible look.

Edmonton, Canada: June 1996

That's not how the story goes! said Cleopatra Maria energetically, licking sauce from her lips, taking another bite from her burrito. She chewed and talked and chewed, her cheeks full of refried beans.

That musical is full of shit! Annie Taylor was in her sixties when she went over Niagara Falls, said Cleopatra Maria and she waved her arm over her head like it was a barrel going over a waterfall.

Cleopatra Maria dribbled sauce on the front of her blouse. She tried to wipe herself with a paper napkin and spread the sauce onto her lap. Waldmann the third family dachshund licked her thigh where the sauce dripped.

If I made that kind of mess when I ate, I'd be locked up, said Clotilde.

She died in poverty and obscurity in her eighties. I know that for a fact, said Cleopatra Maria.

Good for you honey, to remember all that, said Rosario. Now go change your shirt.

I think you read the wrong book, said Hannelore gently, she had to remember that Cleopatra Maria was so temperamental. The musical says that Anna Edson Taylor married a millionaire hotel owner, said Hannelore, and she died rich and famous. She was not in her sixties when she went over Niagara Falls in a barrel. She was in her twenties. Twenty-nine at the most.

She was too in her sixties! said Cleopatra Maria, and she could feel her head expand from tears. She always started to cry when people didn't listen to her. You think I can't read, Oma? You think just because I'm a girl I don't know what I'm reading? Mum! Tell her to stop being so patronizing.

Mutti, chided Rosario.

Cleopatra Maria has a photographic memory, said Dieter. I have tested her. She remembers details in books exactly as they appear, Mutti.

The musical would not lie! protested Hannelore.

Annie Edson Taylor died of old age! said Cleopatra Maria. Probably pneumonia or something Victorian. I read it in a book! I have the book!

Cleopatra Maria put down her fork and blinked. If she swallowed quickly enough and often enough she could stop the tears from coming. She wanted to put a bag over her head. She was a precious flower, her mother told her every day she was a precious flower before she went to school, but no one was treating her like a precious flower tonight.

Where's the book? said Hannelore. Dieter, did you know about this?

Dieter's mouth was full, he stuffed it with more food and kept stuffing it. The more he stuffed his mouth, the less he had to say. It was his idea they invite his mother for supper on a school night. Rosario would make him pay.

Cleopatra Maria, said Rosario. Why don't you go get the book to show your Oma.

What am I, a servant? snapped Cleopatra Maria, and the tears retreated back into her head. Oma doesn't believe me, why should I bother? She should get it herself.

But Cleopatra Maria slid away from the table. Watched a little television before coming back to the table.

And she was ugly, said Cleopatra Maria. See? Cleopatra Maria fluttered the pages in Hannelore's face. Look at this picture. Face like a boot.

I don't understand, said Hannelore. The musical would not lie. Where are my reading glasses?

Musicals lie all the time, said Dieter. You think the von Trapp family was really singing all the time when they were running away from the Nazis? Who can run like hell and sing like an angel at the same time in real life?

Maybe they had good lungs, said Clotilde.

Well, that certainly was a delicious dinner, said Rosario.

Yes, delicious, said Clotilde.

Wasn't that a good dinner? said Rosario to Cleopatra Maria.

It's giving me zits.

Who's Miss Cranky Boots tonight, said Rosario. Go help your father and Tante with the dishes. Then you can play a game on your new computer, the one Frau Schnadelhuber gave you.

What am I, a servant? said Cleopatra Maria.

That Frau Schnadelhuber, said Hannelore, she's a nut-case. She says she stole that computer can you believe it? Why don't you read the chapter out loud to me, Cleopatra Maria, said Hannelore. And you can tell me some more about Annie Edson Taylor.

After Cleopatra Maria went to bed, Hannelore made Clotilde read and translate the chapter about Anna Taylor out loud to her again. Clotilde was the one who liked the books. In the library every chance she could get.

The Royal Auditorium: June 1996

Hannelore loved *Niagara! the Musical*, loved it so much the white downy hairs on the back of her neck rose from the dry ice, the skin on her forearms sang along with the chorus. Loved it even more now that she knew the truth, Hannelore worshipped the Niagara daredevil Anna Edson Taylor, all of sixty-three, plunging over the giant waterfalls in 1901 in a barrel she practically put together herself to become the Queen of the Mist. Of course in the Musical she was twenty-five at most and ended up marrying a wealthy Niagara Falls hotel owner, but Hannelore now knew the truth.

Sixty-three. Poor, desperate Anna Taylor. Hannelore in her life had never risked any cliffs, never before desired to set herself apart from the wallpaper in her uniforms as housewife, widow, mother. Being the smooth and efficient wallpaper, the carpet pattern no one could remember. They said Hitler used to roll around on the ground and chew the carpets in his rages. The hidden tunnels. Just because she was old didn't mean she didn't have feelings. She wasn't forty years married to the same old lump like Dot. She wasn't getting over a divorce after a fifty-year marriage like Bonnie.

Except for early on during the war, an unmarried life in every way. And was this why she never remarried? She always thought it was because all the men were killed. There were no men left. Anna Taylor also only married once, Anna Taylor was also Anna Edson. Old and fat and poor and unloved. Hannelore old and nearly poor and only provisionally loved. Also fat. Weekend filial love. Dieter's mowing the lawn and nailing shingles to the roof love.

Then there was the show with the understudy when Hannelore's love for Anna Edson Taylor exploded.

From their seats, the best in the house, Hannelore and Dot knew something was wrong when the house-lights went down thirty-five minutes after the show was supposed to start. Annie came out onto the stage rolling her barrel in the opening scene and Hannelore and Dot suddenly wanted someone to wake them from what was obviously going to be a nightmare. Sharon-Lee Silver wasn't leaving out words and yawning behind her hand, Sharon-Lee Silver was no longer Sharon-Lee Silver, her wig was wrong, her hips were wrong and her breasts, her breasts were unwieldy and huge like puddings and wobbled so much they leaked up into her chin and made her whole face into pudding. No amount of make-up caked on the singer's face could hide how old this understudy was. Old. They knew the woman playing Annie Taylor on the stage was not Sharon-Lee Silver at all. Hannelore trembled when the woman opened her mouth and began to sing, no singing like it, no singing like she'd ever heard before.

Drunk, Ida told them during intermission. The stage manager found Sharon-Lee Silver slobbering drunk in her dressing-room from going out to cowboy bars all weekend. So was her understudy, who went with her. Got back late from some all-night rodeo party and they both passed out in the auditorium dressing-room. Hamish says this is the wardrobe mistress on tonight and the producers are furious. She's sixty years old if she's a day, but she's been with the show since the very beginning and knows the part from watching it backstage the whole time.

Her singing voice isn't so bad, said Dot, but she ain't no Sharon-Lee Silver.

Oh well, sighed Ida. Girls will be girls. And young girls do silly things.

You don't have to be a young girl to be drunk and slobbering, said Dot. She busily scooped ice into glasses, the slicing sound of the glass through the ice piled in the sink. You could be as old as my husband, she said. Prime example of drunk and slobbering.

You should leave him, said Ida.

And go where? said Dot. It's his pension keeps us eating and a roof over our heads. I'll manage, Dot said. She scrubbed vigorously at the sparkling metal counter. Besides, she said, I can always just take another antidepressant.

Ida and Hannelore polished wine glasses doubtfully.

The understudy was not Sharon-Lee Silver, but to Hannelore she had a voice like Sacher Torte: deep, thick and painfully chocolate. A voice that ran its fingers through Hannelore's hair and massaged her scalp, penetrated her brain with its warm water sound.

Patrons scampered up and down the aisles. Waved their arms and clucked around the lobby in their expensive suits, their expensive ticket stubs in their hands.

My wife and I paid to see Sharon-Lee Silver, said one in a grey suit. He shook his stub in Hannelore's face, almost jammed the stub up Hannelore's nose. I did not pay eighty dollars to see an understudy who doesn't even look the *part*, he shouted.

At least if I'd been *told*, said a woman in a red fur coat, also with an expensive stub. But I wasn't even told!

Patrons shook their programmes and fingers in the faces of the ushers who ran around like hens in a barnyard. Patrons stormed the office of the Management at intermission wanting Sharon-Lee Silver or their money *back*.

No, the wardrobe mistress wasn't Sharon-Lee Silver, didn't have the pointy toes and the flutey voice; the wardrobe mistress was too heavy, her voice stirred too far below the changing lights, the dry ice, the painted backdrop. Sharon-Lee Silver's voice was as fluffy and pretty as her wig and she sang about how to live happily ever after. The wardrobe woman's voice told about being alone, about poverty and death. This Annie Edson Taylor was too real. No one wanted to pay eighty dollars to see an old and bitter woman tell the world like it was, how she had no place because no one would give her any room. The woman on the stage could have been any of them: Bonnie, Ida, Dot, even Hannelore. Even Hannelore.

At the end of the show Hannelore's eyes were red and swollen with excitement, with disappointment. Dot patted her on the arm in the dark, said: You o.k.?

But Hannelore melted into the wallpaper, sank into the floor until all the patrons and other ushers had left. She fiddled with her shoes, her nylons, stood alone in her coat at the door to the tunnels under the stage. The beige coat with the mended hole in the right pocket. She twirled her scarf around her head, once around her neck and looked into the dark. A grey scarf. Grey and beige. Her white hair and her coat, the coat with the mended hole in the right pocket. Hannelore mended the hole with beige thread, thread that matched her coat, she was very lucky to find the thread otherwise she would have had to give away the coat. Her beige coat, her hair silver in the dark, she touched the scarf on her head, the hole in her pocket, dug her eyes into Annie's set-barrel, cat's claws into the wooden arms of a couch.

You wanna go over Niagara Falls, you don't go in one of those, said Hamish. The baseball cap. The kilt.

Pardon me? said Hannelore.

Electric sweat on Hannelore's forehead, in her armpits, under and between her breasts. Blinkers on her eyes. All she could see was The Lighting Man. The tunnel. Hamish.

I said, you wanna go over Niagara Falls, you don't go in a dinky piece of wood like that one.

People have done it and survived.

Pure luck. Now, *I've* got a barrel, I've got one that could take on the Falls and then jump into outer space. Wanna see it?

I don't believe you—Hamish.

She would have liked to feel his last name with her tongue, but his first name dropped to the ground between them like a rabbit without ears.

She extended a hand to shake. She was afraid to touch him, but this was the polite thing to do. The most appropriate choice for the situation.

You a Kraut?

Hannelore put her hand back in her coat pocket.

I am no Kraut. I am not a weed, you filthy man.

Gotta sister in Germany. In Munich.

The south. How boring. Every German in this country seems to come from Bavaria.

You from the south?

Certainly not.

Wanna see it? said Hamish.

Certainly not, said Hannelore and she tried to swish him away like a fly. The more he talked, the more he drained the sad beauty from the evening.

Hamish pulled off the tarp. Hannelore eyed his heavy, hairy calves nervously.

Very nice, said Hannelore politely.

Nice. That's not a very descriptive word, said Hamish. You could do better than that.

A very fine ball, said Hannelore.

Time to go now, she thought.

That's right. A ball, said Hamish. The Niagara Ball. Modelled after the Plunge-O-Sphere used by William Fitzgerald a.k.a. Nathan T. Boya to go over the Falls in '61. Weighted at the bottom, layer of ping-pong balls inside the outside layer of super-rubber for buoyancy. Trap door. Slides open and closed, see? That way there's a better seal to keep water out. Rubber instead of hard plastic because rubber has more give and won't crash in. Bolt on the door's flush with the surface so you don't get locked in and the bolt won't get knocked off at impact. You can open it from the inside *and* the outside. Guy who helped me make it was a German. He had some head for gadgets. But Germans always have heads for gadgets.

Hamish walked around the Niagara Ball, taller than him, wider than him, he ran his hands over its smooth, bright orange sides like he wanted to eat it. Not a perfect ball, but an egg, the surface a rubbery day-glo orange. A door, a head shorter than Hannelore, at the side with the elaborate bolt system. The egg glowed in the dark of the tunnels. Hannelore could smell the rubbery-plastic newness of the egg. A brand new egg-shaped car.

But why would you make this thing? said Hannelore. What's the point?

Because one day, I'll make this baby sing. Push her over Niagara Falls, make myself a million bucks, get in the Guiness world book of records.

When?

What? said Hamish.

When will you go?

Me go? I wouldn't go! The ball's going! I'll put in a cat or something. A dog maybe, whadda you think I am? Crazy? Wanna check the inside? Look inside.

There is nothing very heroic about pushing over a cat, said Hannelore.

Well *I* couldn't go in it, my stomach would explode.

Hannelore bent her head and stepped carefully through the narrow trap door into the claustrophobic darkness of the Niagara Ball, the smell of what felt like puffy upholstery covering the interior walls. Dark and small, like locking herself inside a large trunk. Hamish squeezed in after her, his big belly pushed into her side, she knocked her head against a wall and dislodged her bow tie. Dark, dark and small and only the filtered light through the tiny window above her head, at the small tip of the egg.

Got style, eh? he said. Picked out the colour upholstery myself.

Enough, she said, crammed against the interior wall by his stomach, his breath. I can't see anything. I want to get out.

But you haven't seen the console, look I've put in lights, extra air pockets!

Hamish jammed a button behind her head and a tiny light blinked on.

I've engineered it so the Ball's super lightweight, a special light-weight rubber, a baby could lift it! That way it's over the rails and swimming before the cops can put down their doughnuts! Hamish said, his voice excited like a boy's, his breath smelling like old cabbage and cigarette butts. She could smell the ripeness of his armpits as he reached around her to press buttons, pull straps.

Special adjustable harnesses to keep the bodies inside it from being thrown around, he said. Like in a moving-truck see? Seatbelts. Window so's you can see where you're going, made of special plexi-glass. Me and my buddy were gonna use it, then we decided to do the cat instead.

Poor cat, said Hannelore. Cruelty to animals.

Nothing cruel about it. Probably the most exciting thing the cat'll ever do. Beats the hell outta smokin' catnip.

Hannelore touched a harness hanging from one of the sides and accidentally banged her elbow into his stomach.

I'm thinking I could even fit a cd player in here, he said. What do you think? Hannah?

Hannelore hid her repulsion at his smell. Ida must have told him her name. Very nice, she said.

Suddenly his body went still.

You know I always was in love with Greta Garbo, he said. You look kinda like her. He leaned his face in to hers. His breath in her face, nowhere to move.

Really. She was Swedish. Very nice meeting you Mr. Hamish, Hannelore said and thought about shaking his hand, then thought, Forget it.

You will have to get out first, Mr. Hamish, your stomach is in the way.

You ever been to Niagara Falls? You ever looked at the water? Really looked at it? asked Hamish. His voice was high like he was about to cry.

Hannelore's stomach jumped. Crying men upset her. Men were

not supposed to cry. Men crying reminded her of the war.

I guess not, he said. He wiped his nose on the side of his hand.

He squeezed himself out the door.

Niagara Falls? whispered Hannelore in the dark with Hamish The Lighting Man in the tunnels under the stage of the Royal Auditorium, the biggest auditorium west of Manitoba. Of course I have looked at the water, she said. I know all about the water.

Hannelore's eyebrow twitched, Anna Edson Taylor's nervous sweat suddenly transferred to her upper lip.

I love that water, said Hamish, even more quietly. He held his hand out to her to help her from the vessel.

Hannelore's hands moved towards Hamish's hand with the quick, methodical paddle of froglegs.

She leaned forward to squeeze herself out and he kissed her in the doorway of the Niagara Ball. She kissed him back.

To this day nobody really knows what possessed William Fitzgerald to invest his life savings in a "Plunge-O-Sphere" so he could conquer the Falls. . . . His words when he was taken from his odd craft in July 1961 give some hint as to his intentions. "I have integrated the Falls," he said. That was the only reference to his colour.

—PIERRE BERTON, Niagara: A History of the Falls

The next night Sharon-Lee Silver's face looked as animated as a salmon fillet, but she did her job. The audience got their eighty dollars' worth, and the producers could only frown in their expensive suits when Sharon-Lee Silver made an unchoreographed clutch at her hungover forehead partway through "My hands and feet are ee-lec-tric." But the audience got their money's worth so nothing mattered, not Sharon-Lee Silver's headache and sick alcohol stomach, nor the freshly sacked understudy sobbing in the dressing-room. The technicians bumped around hopelessly like grasshoppers with their legs pulled off praying for their jobs. Even the Auditorium's Management felt the strain and had a board meeting catered by the city's most expensive Greek restaurant to discuss what changes could be made for smoother running of the Auditorium. One senior executive suggested they fire all the old women and hire prettier ushers. Then he ate his spanikopita.

You know, said Dot. I don't think Sharon-Lee Silver is so great after all. I think she's overrated. Let's go to the lobby.

Yes, said Hannelore.

Hannelore wrinkled her nose at Sharon-Lee Silver's pointy-toed, spoiled diva performance, the dark green odour from Dot's feet as Dot slipped her stockinged feet back into her sandals and gathered her bag of wool and needles.

Hannelore & Clotilde's House: July 1996

Hannelore realized she hadn't been with a man in so long she didn't know how they worked anymore. She worried that she didn't remember how her own body worked anymore. Not that she was ever going to put herself in that kind of position with The Lighting Man, no, she would never do that.

Sometimes Hannelore's brain forced her to imagine what Clotilde and Frau Schnadelhuber did when Hannelore was not in the house. The whole thing popped into Hannelore's brain: first the image of Clotilde's empty bed, then Clotilde in the bed, then Frau Schnadelhuber beside Clotilde in the bed, the two of them together in Clotilde's bed and the first imaginings of what they did together in that bed when Hannelore wasn't in the house to interfere made Hannelore drop a whole pile of programmes, sometimes a whole bucket of ice on the new lobby carpet. She tried to focus on Cleopatra Maria, coming over every second day, every weekend, looking to be entertained and in need of direction. Hannelore tried to focus on being a grandmother.

Everyone hates me, said Cleopatra Maria in her chair, a towel draped over her head for no particular reason.

Have some more sausage, said Hannelore. It will make you feel better.

Can't, said her grandchild. Cholesterol. It's never too early to watch your cholesterol, especially when you're on the Pill.

The Pill? thought Hannelore. Bury this thought.

You know, the Birth Control Pill, said Cleopatra Maria loudly from under her towel. So that I don't get pregnant from having so much sex. I have an incredibly active sex life. Speaking of which—

Cleopatra Maria took a small plastic disk out of her pocket. She turned the wheel on the disk and a Birth Control Pill dropped into the palm of her hand. Cleopatra Maria popped the Pill into her mouth.

There, she said. Now I can tell all my lovers not to worry. I have everything under control. You don't have to worry about *me*, Oma.

Cleopatra Maria didn't have an active sex life, she had no sex life at all. She used to have a sort of sex life. She and Niven, a lab technician at the university, used to do every sexual thing they could while still keeping their pants on. They'd fool around in the back room where the medical department kept the human corpses, the smell of formaldehyde her special aphrodisiac, but Niven was a long time ago. She thought of Niven and his stupid lab coat. Niven and his premature ejaculations. Niven shooting off like a rocket when she just touched his elbow or spoke too closely in his ear.

For example, she'd say, I need another Petri dish, and touch his arm, and Niven would suddenly look at her like a silly sheep and she'd know he'd just ejaculated into his pants.

It's the way you smell, Niven said, and then he'd scurry off to the bathroom to clean himself up.

Niven perpetually brimming with sperm, she had to let him go, she couldn't afford to get pregnant at this point in her career even though she valued his brain. Niven was a genius, she was a genius, and like most geniuses, they were terrible at understanding themselves, their bodies, basic things like tying up shoelaces, they stunk at interacting socially with other people not in their field of study.

Even though Cleopatra Maria and Niven never took their pants off, even though she knew it was physiologically impossible without super-bullet sperm, she still freaked out when she thought of the sperm maybe soaking through his underpants, his jeans, her jeans, her underpants, and maybe, just maybe, Niven's sperm finding their spermish way to her uterus. The day she found out he wasn't wearing any underwear at all, Niven became ancient history. She also stopped going swimming in salt-water pools and hot springs. What if sperm were floating in the water and somehow found their way inside her? Men like Niven who had no control over their bodies, oozing, leaking, spitting, crying sperm.

Sperm in saliva, snot, urine, faeces, sweat, ear wax, and Cleopatra Maria sharing the same water, the same air with all these perpetually leaking human bags of sperm. Cleopatra Maria would make a terrible mother, and she knew she'd go mad if she had an abortion. She took the Birth Control Pill just in case because you never knew about toilet seats in public washrooms, under-chlorinated swimming pool water. She took the Pills like vitamins and every time she got her period, felt the menstrual ache and squishiness of the thickened blood messing up her underpants, she dissolved with relief because the blood dribbled on her sheets and the toilet seat meant there would be no Cleopatra Maria Jr. starting to split its cells in Cleopatra Maria's womb this month.

So her fear of impregnation was not logical. But like any genius in her situation, she couldn't help herself.

It was hell being a woman.

Hannelore watched Cleopatra Maria put the small plastic wheel of Birth Control Pills into her pocket. Hannelore zoomed from the room with the plates.

Hannelore didn't need this information about Cleopatra Maria, but it was good that they were sharing. This was a Canadian, Canadian spelled with a "C," thing, sharing so much. The Pill. Hannelore turned on the water in the sink.

Are you listening to me, Oma? called Cleopatra Maria from her chair, from under her towel. Aren't you worried that I'm a teenage nymphomaniac in need of guidance! Don't you wish you'd had a grandson instead of a granddaughter looking to get knocked up because that's how all girls end up eventually! I'm nothing but a girl-burden!! she screamed.

Hannelore thought about Pills. Thought about how she'd never seen Cleopatra Maria with a boy ever. Chewed on Cleopatra Maria's leftover Bratwurst skin, her head hurting from the shout-

134

ing. She wished she had a towel for her own head. Hannelore remembered she had to take her after-dinner pills.

No, Hannelore would continue walking the long way around the theatre instead of taking the short cut through the tunnels. She did not want to meet up with him again even though Ida told her he waited for her same as always. The thoughts that popped into her head about Cleopatra Maria's Pills, her perverted sister, the television crammed with kissing and naked bodies, she would ignore all of these things.

So when Hamish tipped his baseball cap at her for the fourth time that week like they had never met, he was coy like a young girl, she was suddenly very fed up with him being a coy man over sixty trying to pretend he was a coy girl. If his coyness continued she would be dead and buried before he made any concrete advances at all. When he silently tipped his hat goodnight to her, she stopped and stood very still and stared at him. She stood and waited for him to do something. She breathed heavily like she had just run a marathon and now had to stand still waiting for a tardy city bus. The woman confronting the man was not how courting was done when she was a girl, only the girls with loose morals chased so blatantly after the men, but she remembered that she was no longer a girl, she had to be forward because all the men had lost their spines, their resolve, and this man was especially spineless. She suspected pollutants in the air were responsible for this race of spineless men.

Well? she said.

Well, he cleared his throat.

Well aren't you going to court me?

What? he said stupidly.

Hannelore pushed Hamish backwards with her very sweaty hands. She pushed him and pushed him until she had pushed him onto his Niagara Ball, and then she pushed him not just with her hands, but with her fat, old woman's body and her out-of-practice mouth.

Excuse me, he said.

He reached behind him and opened the trap door. He scrambled into the Ball and reached out his hand for her. She graciously accepted his hand and squeezed in next to him.

At first to ease the tension, she pretended she was a teenage nymphomaniac on Pills starring in her own show on television. That was the easiest way. Then she remembered how men worked no problem.

In the tunnels, in the dark, Hannelore under Hamish's kilt. It was a scene so momentous it should have gone on the wall in Hannelore's sitting room next to all the other family photos.

Unfortunately, no one had a camera.

In the morgue lay the latest suicide. . . . The furious pummelling of the Upper Rapids followed by the plunge over Horseshoe Falls and the rock-to-rock banging through the Lower Rapids into the Whirlpool had left the tragic victim without hair, without face and without even fingers from which prints could be taken.

—ANDY O'BRIEN, Daredevils of Niagara

Hamish liked his lunch at exactly twelve.

Watches don't tell the time, he said. My stomach do.

Hannelore was happy when she watched him eat enough for ten men, she fingered the leftover burn on her top lip from Hamish's whiskers and watched him begin to eat, the spurt of sausage juice up the metal of the fork, the wide Hamish mouth opening to receive the food, the creamed kohlrabi disappearing down his gigantic Hamish throat.

I am falling in love, she thought.

Or into the most disgusting lust possible.

Clotilde and Frau Schnadelhuber let him take the best chair, but she watched them turn the volume control in their heads way down when he talked. Their inner eyelids closed like cats', the membranes in their ears descended the moment he began to speak, but still they didn't leave the room, they could have left the room but they didn't, Hannelore should have just kicked them out of the room so she could have him all to herself, but she also wanted to show him *off*. Clotilde and Frau Schnadelhuber had been trained to appreciate men, even if they had nothing to do with men. They couldn't help themselves, they had to stay in the room. Men were important. But so was volume control.

Hamish didn't wear the baseball cap in the house.

Frau Schnadelhuber in her Dirndl, Hamish in his kilt, and Cleopatra Maria had started wearing a kente cloth and a bitchy teenage mouth every Sunday. The sitting-room was a veritable international summit.

I like my lunch at twelve, said Hamish.

At *twelve*, said Hamish.

You could cook it yourself, said Cleopatra Maria not even turning her head away once from the television set. Then you wouldn't have to worry about it not being on time. What are you Oma, a servant?

Cleopatra Maria's fingers tapped the keyboard of her laptop computer absent-mindedly while she watched television. Every so often she would jot a number down in her notebook with her silver mechanical pencil.

What are you doing? asked Hamish.

Calculating the odds of an alien spacecraft landing on the roof of this building and beaming you up into oblivion.

Is she adopted? said Hamish. She must get her bad temper from her biological parents.

No, said Hannelore.

Cleopatra Maria spat on the floor in the direction of Hamish.

Hannelore noticed Cleopatra Maria was in no hurry to make her own lunches. Cleopatra Maria just turned on the television, doodled on her computer and in her notebook, and complained to the air about her pimples.

Hannelore changed the sheets on the bed often. Whenever he came over in fact. The smell.

She ignored Clotilde's comments, Clotilde's sticking her tongue out like a reptile and wiggling it in the air.

Go read a communist pamphlet, said Hannelore. Go find yourself a newspaper and leave me alone.

You're so relaxed these days, Hannelore, said Clotilde, and Hannelore felt the blood rush to her head and pop out her ears in heart-shaped droplets.

So relaxed, said Clotilde. You're like a different person. You even walk differently, an extra swing in your step. Like when you saw Freddy in concert that time in 1972.

Enough, said Hannelore, and she took her hearing aid out of her ear and set it on the cabinet.

One day Hannelore said to Hamish: Your stomach watch is fast.

No, said Hamish, Lunch is late.

Lunch is *not* late, she said, and her nose wrinkled unpleasantly at his smell, his skewed Kanadian-Scottish sense of time. Her hearing aid whistled from the sudden tension in her jaws.

And Krauts are supposed to be so punctual, said Hamish, his filthy Lighting Man hands on her good linen tablecloth.

I am not a weed, you filthy man, Hannelore said, and I am *always* punctual.

By then lunch was exactly two minutes late.

Hannelore resentfully watched him chew his food and instead of offering him the last of the salad in the delicious dressing she always prepared herself, she ate the last of the salad herself, ate the lettuce and tomatoes and chopped circles of green onion, ate the shallow, sweet pool of salad dressing on the bottom of the bowl with a soup spoon. Waste not want not. From old make new.

The spoon was a silver one, silver warm and dull in her mouth, the edge only vaguely sharp. It was older than she, one of her mother's spoons, her mother died before Hannelore even met Heinrich and suddenly Hannelore remembered her mother, their mother's smell, her clean competent hands, the oily black of her pupils. Her wooden spoons. The crumbling war bread, so crumbly it wasn't bread at all. Dirty Scottish hands on a clean tablecloth? Never.

Hannelore licked the spoon clean. She would lick the bowl too. Good food not to waste. If only there was someone who would lick Hamish clean, including the inside of his head. She was too old to be dating her father.

The sex wasn't so wonderful anyway. It made her feel perverted, he wanted it in the middle of the day when she preferred it later in the dark—in the Niagara Ball was the best. She couldn't walk around naked in front of a stranger, she didn't even take off her clothes to bathe hardly, but he was always pulling them off, pulling them off, trying to pull them all off. Her husband was much cleaner, more efficient, none of this insistence on nakedness, no messing around with his tongue in strange places, everything over in three minutes instead of the hours Hamish insisted on. She was not nineteen years old. She was not prepared for gymnastics at her age.

She did not have hours to waste in bed.

Sex schmex, she said to herself. Sex schmex.

This sex did not schmeck, she said to herself and laughed. Her bed could stay clean forever if she wanted it to. Now that his filthy toenails had been banished.

So her relationship with Hamish was over. Over. No more Hamish. Yes. He would leave with his show whenever and she wouldn't? have to see him anymore hanging out in the tunnels instead of doing his job. She was free.

So then there was Hamish. So she changed her mind sometimes.

When they were not together in the Niagara Ball or soiling her boiled sheets because she'd changed her mind and needed to remind herself why she had changed her mind in the first, second, and third place, Hamish reminded Hannelore of Dieter pulling extra-long blades of grass from Waldmann the dachshund's bottom. The problem with Hamish was that Hamish in his kilt, his breath like compost, also reminded her of that special melt of between the between, reminded her of the rush of Niagara Falls, the cool, chlorine smell of Sunday mornings at the swimming pool, the overwhelming warmth of natural hot springs in the mountains.

How to reconcile repulsion and battery-recharging at the same time? Her instincts told her that she should marry him now that she had been with him in his barrel. Barrelling around the barrel. Not a barrel. The thought of marrying again at her age made Hannelore laugh. Or was this the lust Clotilde had been telling Hannelore about for years, the conversations between Frau Schnadelhuber and Clotilde that made Hannelore put her hands over her ears because some things about her sister Hannelore just didn't want to know, because some things should be left private between husband and wife or whatever, because some things made Hannelore so jealous Hannelore wanted to drown herself over and over?

I need sex, Clotilde used to say periodically. I don't care how old I get, I will always need the sex. I am going to find myself some sex.

Hannelore would take out her hearing-aid, turn up the television set.

And now Ida and Dot and the other ushers. Screaming like a cage full of parrots.

Is he your boyfriend? whispered Dot, her toes wiggling in the dark.

I won't tell anyone, whispered Ida. You can tell me.

You want me to wait for you? asked Bonnie, her coat in her hands. I can wait for you and we can walk to the train station together. You shouldn't be hanging out in the tunnels by yourself like that. I can wait for you. Or maybe you're getting a ride from Hamish?

Hamish's cigars did not bother Hannelore, nor the fact that his teeth were as brown and long as the cigars, nor the fact that he was fifteen years younger, nor the wrinkly, perpetually red skin on the back of his neck, the hairs sprouting from his ears and nose, the magnificence of his round belly and large, scarred, competent hands. It was the smell that bothered Hannelore. Only the smell. What a ridiculous reason to reject a man: because of his smell. Hannelore was lucky a man was even interested in her.

But the smell was familiar: garden sheds, her father's lectures about punctuality, about how he wished he'd had sons instead of useless lumps of daughters. Men's smells, how to describe them? Sometimes Clotilde smelled like a man, when she was being stubborn, but never so strong. The set of Papa's elbows on the table as he waited for his daughters to lay down the Mittagessen. Rosario also sat on her bottom like Hannelore's father, as if the world was meant to clean up after her. When Hannelore first saw Rosario sitting, reading the tv guide in the leftover mess of the diningroom table, Hannelore was disgusted, now she wondered if maybe it wasn't right that once in a while a woman should take a little rest. Although men in the kitchen were incompetent. This was a scientific fact. Dieter made bread all right, but not fine bread like a woman could.

By now she knew what she wanted from Hamish, but it had nothing to do with lunches on time, nothing to do with the monster under his kilt. Everything to do with the moisture between the between. Her moisture could help Hannelore tell the future. Water swirling around her but not touching her, Hannelore shouting her presence to the world, not a suicide just add water, but desire. The desire to *be* the water, the movement, to be inside her own living, pumping heart.

The Royal Auditorium: August 1996

Thank you for the tickets, rumbled Clotilde. They stood by the mini waterfall in the lobby, the tiny barrels bouncing among the machine-made waves and underwater lights.

Those were good seats, said Hannelore.

We know, said Clotilde. You told us. You keep telling us. They were good seats, but still my back hurts. My knees feel like hell.

A very nice show, said Frau Schnadelhuber politely, she shook Hannelore's hand thank you.

Truthfully, Frau Schnadelhuber hardly watched the show, she was too busy trying not to scream from pleasure from Clotilde's hand under her skirt in the dark. Still after almost ten years, Frau Schnadelhuber's brain went straight to between her legs when she was with Clotilde. And this is what love is like, thought Frau Schnadelhuber looking at Clotilde dressed in her iron-grey cardigan and wool skirt in the middle of summer. Love was like a pool of lava that bubbled through her eyes and nose and the cracks between her fingers. It was like driving the fastest German car ever made, Frau Schnadelhuber sped on the Trans-Canada highway, the Autobahn, the winding highways, the warmth of the steering wheel between her fingers, the growling of the engine and the movement over the packed tar and asphalt.

Being with Clotilde was like getting her driver's license renewed: Class "L" for Love. Frau Schnadelhuber snapped on her driving goggles, wound her white silk scarf around her throat, and sped off into the horizon with her love at one thousand kilometres an hour. She did not believe such happiness.

Then there was being with Karl. Like dragging a ten-tonne cart with square wheels.

Karl's best story was that he used to chew tar as a child growing up. Pick it from the street in Northern Alberta, he and his sister. They would tell the tar story at Christmas dinners over the turkey and then laugh and laugh like it was the funniest thing ever. Frau Schnadelhuber would go to the kitchen and fiddle with something, anything she could find, push the button down on the toaster, gush water into the kettle, just so she didn't have to hear the stupid tar story again while she was trying to eat. The worst was him telling this story when they were having their one-sided sex, before she kicked him out of her bed for good, because then there was no kitchen to escape to. No wonder they were such horrible people, he and his sister, eating tar off the street. The tar went straight to their skulls and deposited itself in the middle of their brains.

Frau Schnadelhuber never chewed tar, she drove over tar. The dangers of Tar and Love were the same.

But did you understand the show, said Hannelore.

Of course we understood it! burst out Clotilde. What do you think we are, stupid? We need to find a taxi.

But don't you think it's interesting? said Hannelore. The woman going over the Niagara Falls in a barrel? Isn't a sixty-three-year-old woman going over Niagara Falls in a barrel inspiring?

Sixty-three? She couldn't have been more than twenty!

But in real life she was sixty-three, said Hannelore. Sixty-three years old in 1901! In 1901!

Clotilde fell asleep during the second half of the show. Too much singing, she had never been one for so much singing, she was only interested in the special effects. She was not interested in obviously beautiful young women with guaranteed happy endings doing idiotic things. She also maybe shouldn't have drunk that gin and tonic so fast during the intermission.

Clotilde remembered reading out loud from Cleopatra Maria's book about Niagara Falls. Oh yes, I remember, sixty-three, she said. Where is the bar?

The bar is closed. It doesn't stay open after the show. What are you, an alcoholic? said Hannelore.

I forgot she was sixty-three, said Clotilde. That's a better story. Why didn't they stick to that story?

That's what I think! said Hannelore. One night there was a sixty-year-old woman playing her. That was the finest performance.

Sixty, thought Frau Schnadelhuber. Frau Schmitt's bow tie is crooked.

If she could do it, we could do it, said Hannelore.

We can't sing! Have a nice ride, said Clotilde rudely, and she held out her arm for Frau Schnadelhuber.

I think we should go visit them, said Hannelore.

Well yes, said Clotilde. We could visit them again. Next year, said Clotilde and she looked at Frau Schnadelhuber. Next year you could go?

I've never been to Niagara Falls, said Frau Schnadelhuber.

They are majestic, said Clotilde, and the sound of "s" in "majestic" made Frau Schnadelhuber shift the gears of her car to super-cruise control.

Not next year. Sooner, said Hannelore.

Whatever, said Clotilde.

Whatever, thought Frau Schnadelhuber.

This year, said Hannelore.

All right, this year, said Clotilde. This year? asked Clotilde and she looked at Frau Schnadelhuber, who blushed and pressed her hands together over her Dirndl apron.

Hannelore realized they just didn't get it, they didn't understand, Anna Taylor was lost on them. She was disappointed in Clotilde's denseness. Frau Schnadelhuber was an oversexed vegetable, Hannelore could smell the sex on Frau Schnadelhuber's mind and she wanted to clap on a gas mask to stop the stench.

Why was Hannelore the only one who understood why Annie

Taylor did it? All about choices and having no choices. All about shouting your presence to the world. I am not invisible. I deserve eye contact and to be taken seriously. Clotilde, on the other hand, always used her cane in airports even when she didn't need it just so young women would rush at her with airport wheelchairs, offering to wheel her around.

Annie Edson Taylor tested her barrel before going over herself, she put a cat in the barrel and sent it over the Horseshoe Falls. The cat died hideously, yowled in Annie's ears for years afterwards, but even though the cat died, Annie decided to go over anyway. She did it anyway because there was simply *no choice*. Holding on with all your fingers, sinews stretched like rubber bands over the gorge that yawned poverty and almshouses and loneliness and women who were nothing but bags of flesh to be shut away as burdens. This wasn't about suicide, it was about grabbing life by the balls and pulling until they snapped.

Hannelore hurried to the tunnels, opened the Ball and strapped herself inside.

"I've done what no other woman in the world had the nerve to do . . . only to become a pauper."

That was in February 1921. She was eighty-three years old but was now stubbornly insisting that she was only fifty-seven and in the prime of life. The terrible pounding she took during the barrel trip, she said, had caused her to age prematurely.

—PIERRE BERTON, *Niagara: A History of the Falls*

Niagara Falls, Canada: Thursday, October 24, 1996: 6:12 A.M.

Frau Schnadelhuber's hands haven't stopped shaking since she got in the vessel, nerves weakened by too much life happening to her all at once. So today she is going to die. Today, the day of her death. She has lived through the World Wars one and two, too many air-raids to count, chauffeuring a master spy, detention in a work camp, buried bomb defusal, and now she is going to die simply because she has agreed to throw herself over a cliff. She worries the undertaker won't do her hair right, Hedwig will make sure they do the hair right. Of course, Frau Schnadelhuber is taking for granted that she will still have a head when her body is dredged up from the water.

Hedwig.

Her precious Hedwig. Her precious, selfish Hedwig would kill her mother if she knew where Frau Schnadelhuber was now. Water and noise and jolting, Hedwig would scream at the mess Frau Schnadelhuber is making of her life, spending so much time with these nutty sisters.

Frau Schnadelhuber remembers her eightieth birthday, Hedwig's surprise.

Frau Schnadelhuber undid the bow from the gift bag and pulled out a crinkled ball of purple tissue paper. Her hands trembled a little. Today she was excited: she loved presents, she loved the colour purple. She unwound the tissue paper from around the present, careful not to rip the paper. Later, she would smooth the wrinkles out of the tissue paper, fold the paper neatly, and put it in the cabinet drawer with the rest of her used wrapping paper.

Look Mutti, a Lifeline pendant! said Hedwig.

A pendant for around Frau Schnadelhuber's neck in case she fell and knocked herself out. Press a button and the ambulance men come running.

You can also get a model that looks like a watch if you don't like the pendant. I think a pendant looks nicer.

Hedwig tried to ignore the frown on her mother's face.

This way I don't have to worry about you when I'm not with you, said Hedwig.

Frau Schnadelhuber smoothed out the tissue paper with her fingers, then the palms of her hands.

I am not old enough for this thing, said Frau Schnadelhuber, her palms smoothing the paper. You call this a birthday present? What about some Belgian chocolate? I'm running low on Camels, see my last four packages, they'll be gone in four days, you could have bought me a stick of Camels. That would have been a far better present. Lifeline pendants. Next you'll break my leg so you can buy me a cane.

In her head, Frau Schnadelhuber wondered at Hedwig: Hedwig is trying to make me old. She is trying to make me a burden.

Hedwig hid her disappointment and hurt feelings with a ringing lecture about sugar, smoking, blood pressure and cholesterol, and how bad bacon fat sandwiches were for the system.

I'd offer you a cigarette now that you're done, said Frau Schnadelhuber, but as you can see, I am down to my last four packages and I have none to *spare*.

Hedwig gasped. Put her hands on her hips.

How *dare* Hedwig criticize Frau Schnadelhuber's bacon fat sandwiches. Bacon fat sandwiches. Heaven. Open-faced, the leftover fat from the bacon smeared on a slice of rye bread, and a bit of salt sprinkled over the top. Yes heaven. Angels, harps and halos are bacon fat sandwiches. Frau Schnadelhuber refused to waste fat.

I am hungry, said Frau Schnadelhuber.

She put the pendant back in the fancy gift-bag.

I am hungry, time for you to leave, grumbled Frau Schnadelhuber to Hedwig. Frau Schnadelhuber lit one of her very last cigarettes and blew the smoke high into the air, a rising column of smoke, the smell of security and high-priced living.

But this is my house, said Hedwig. It's my house.

Oh yes.

Frau Schnadelhuber gathered together her things and puffed at her cigarette. In fifteen minutes she would put on her coat and leave for work. Tonight she would stay at Clotilde and Hannelore's house.

There were times a mother had to stick up for her rights, there were times a mother had to proclaim personhood. Frau Schnadelhuber worked five days a week, eight hours a day, she was not an invalid, she was not invisible, no one's burden, she worked for her keep, always had, she would not be thrust into someone's closet and forgotten along with the old photograph albums. No one had to worry about her.

She would do her job and then go have a lot of good quality sex with her lover. And a smoke. A whole pack of smokes in a row.

It's not good to stay with someone because you pity them Hedwig, said Frau Schnadelhuber. Frau Schnadelhuber's lips tugged at her cigarette.

You think I stay with you because I pity you? said Hedwig. Hedwig sniffed. Stiff as a board, that daughter.

I wasn't talking about us, said Frau Schnadelhuber. I meant your father. That's the reason I stayed with him for all those years through all that bullshit. But I also mean you. I don't want you paying attention to me and caring about me because you feel *obligated* to. I want you to be around for real, or just get out.

I could say the same for you, said Hedwig.

Tears pricked Frau Schnadelhuber's eyes. Let's be buried side by side, she said.

Wearing nothing but our brassieres, said Hedwig and she wiped her eyes with the back of her hand.

Too bad your father made me throw out my brassiere collection, said Frau Schnadelhuber. You know that when I died they would have all gone straight to you. Such a collection, some were works of art let me tell you, I took good care of them, even the oldest were in very good shape. Maybe you could have sold them to an underwear museum or somewhere, gotten a little money for them. I hear there is an underwear museum in Belgium, or maybe that is just an interesting rumour. But your father, that oversexed asshole.

He made you throw them out.

Yes. Insecure about his own little pee-pee so I am not supposed to have had a sex life either. But at least I have you. Maybe when I die, you could go find that underwear museum and light a candle for me?

Oh Mama, I would do anything for you.

My daughter my daughter, said Frau Schnadelhuber, and they hugged, two pairs of exquisite breasts pressed against each other like four pancakes.

Frau Schnadelhuber walked jauntily with her very big purse over her shoulder, but inside, worried over how much the pendant must have cost. She would really have preferred cigarettes and chocolate. She worried that Hedwig didn't think she could take care of herself.

That afternoon, the day after the Niagara Falls show, Frau Schnadelhuber lost her job.

Frau Schnadelhuber feels the pressure of Clotilde's body beside her in the half-dark and she thinks about Clotilde, Clotilde's gorgeous heart, Frau Schnadelhuber wants to kiss Clotilde on the lips right now, but she only smells Clotilde in the half-dark, mostly dark, the safety-harnesses hold them together but apart. The jolting and jerking of the vessel throw them together, then apart.

August 1996

Hamish and Hannelore stared at each other over the scraped-clean Mittagessen plates. Hamish licked his lips.

All right! shouted Hamish. I'll show you.

He pushed himself away from the table, spread his legs and began a half-hearted jig.

I knew it, said Hannelore, leaning her head in her hand. You're only a fake Scotsman. Can you even play the bagpipes?

I can draw them with a pencil, said Hamish, and he sat down again, exhausted.

Have another beer, she said. You deserve it.

I have no job, said Frau Schnadelhuber. She stubbed out her cigarette and lit a new one.

The Madame laid me off, she said. I was fired. Forty years I worked at that job and a one-page fax tells me I'm no longer needed. That I should gather my things together. No severance pay no nothing. How am I supposed to live?

The fax said Oma Hupfel was allowed to stay because she looked the most German out of all of us, said Frau Schnadelhuber. Hupfel was on tv so somehow she's better than me! The rest of us, including me who's worked there the longest can just fuck off the fax said and no stealing merchandise on our way out. Hupfel was supposed to *frisk* us as we left the store to make sure we didn't steal anything. How am I supposed to buy groceries? Pay my rent?

Did you take anything? asked Hannelore. She hoped for maybe some links of sausage for tomorrow's supper, thought Frau Schnadelhuber.

Frau Schnadelhuber didn't take anything. The fax stole her life and she had no heart left for stealing.

Move in with your daughter, said Hannelore.

Rest, said Clotilde. And then look for another job.

I am too old to find work. Who would hire me? I have gotten a kick in the pants and in the mouth, said Frau Schnadelhuber and she squeezed her eyes shut. Old and useless, she muttered.

Frau Schnadelhuber smoked and smoked, she put the cigarettes in between her lips and sucked the hot air, her fingers shook as she released the ash from the tips, never before had she realized how complicated it was to smoke, what a true science, no, an art smoking was. The breathing in of the smoke into the lungs, the sitting and swirling of it in the lungs, the blowing through the nose. She once knew a woman who could blow smoke rings from her tear ducts, air and cigarette smoke. In the camp of course. Frau

Schnadelhuber's tear ducts are too clogged with crystallized salt from her dried up tears to allow air for smoke rings.

Frau Schnadelhuber was an artist, a misunderstood artist. She blew a smoke ring bigger than a lasso. The lasso landed around Hannelore's wobbly neck.

The smoke covered the room like a blanket. Spirals and rolls, one long, wide wad of smoke.

Clotilde poured beer for the three of them. Bitburger Pils. Not as good as the beer from where Hannelore and Clotilde grew up, but still very good beer. They were lucky Dieter found it for them.

You could come work as an usher, said Hannelore.

Frau Schnadelhuber cleared her throat and sipped from her glass of beer as if no sound had been made in the room at all.

I need something meaner than beer, said Frau Schnadelhuber.

Scotch? Hannelore's Scotsman always drinks Scotch, said Clotilde.

Scotch, said Hannelore. She took the scotch from the cupboard. Johnnie Walker.

Frau Schnadelhuber grumbled at her small glass of scotch and put the cigarette back in her mouth. She lit another one.

Hannelore grunted and left the room. Frau Schnadelhuber heard the tiny tv in Hannelore's room explode awake.

Clotilde coughed, folded her hands in her lap and waited. She burped. Boiled potatoes.

Clotilde nursed Frau Schnadelhuber through her breakdown after Frau Schnadelhuber lost her job, Clotilde brought her coffee in bed, did her best to arrange Frau Schnadelhuber's hair.

It would be so much more efficient if you just cut it short, like mine, said Clotilde.

Frau Schnadelhuber stared at the seams on the walls under the paint and heard nothing. She wondered what pattern the wallpaper was before someone painted it. Probably Clotilde's nephew, the dog-man. But that was how far gone Frau Schnadelhuber was during the breakdown, obsessed with things like wallpaper, wallpaper was all her shrunken, unemployed brain could handle. Clotilde could have cut Frau Schnadelhuber's hair off, she wouldn't have even noticed.

How is she? asked Hedwig.

Not good, said Clotilde.

Mama come stay with me, said Hedwig. You can sleep in my room. I'll sleep on the couch.

She says she doesn't want to be a burden, said Clotilde from her corner of the room.

Mama, you're not a burden! What would make you think you'd ever be a burden?

Maybe you would put her in a nursing home she says, said Clotilde sideways.

Mama!

She says she could never be in such a place, said Clotilde. I have been in such places. Some are definitely better than others.

Clotilde shrugged her shoulders under her fluffy cardigan.

Maybe if you come back with a stick of Camels next time she'll answer your questions, said Clotilde.

Clotilde and Frau Schmitt's cooking not so great, them being from the North, but Frau Schnadelhuber could hardly taste food, her skin sagging and sticking onto her bones like cellophane in the microwave so she looked like a giant empty grey suitcase. Working with food was supposed to make you less attracted to food, but for forty years food was Frau Schnadelhuber's life. The delicatessen her umbilical cord. Every day she ate lunch from those pans, food she cooked herself, with her heart.

She remained to the end what she had always been—resolute, proud, a little snobbish, and always optimistic. "Through misfortune and other people's dishonesty I lost all my fortune," she said. "It is quite a change for me to come here when I have been used to being entertained in senators' homes in Washington and travelling extensively; but I feel that it is no disgrace and if all my plans materialize, I shall not remain here long."

Two months later, on April 29, she died.

—PIERRE BERTON, Niagara: A History of the Falls

Let's face facts, said Cleopatra Maria in Hamish's general direction (she has watched the lawyers on a lot of lawyer shows and will not deign to look him in the eye. Never let the guilty man think he's your equal), I don't like the way you order my Oma around to make you lunch for twelve o'clock exactly, or the way you suggest in your oh-so-sleazy way that I help her with the dishes you helped mess up. I don't like the way she lets you have the remote control all the time. You get in my way one more time and I'll stick my fork into you like a great big dumpling. Maybe once upon a time men who looked like giant stuffed animals were cute, but nowadays they're just plain annoying. You're as original and appealing as my dandruff problem.

Your grammy doesn't need your help to choose her friends, said Hamish. Don't you have homework to do?

My Oma also hasn't had sex for three million years. She would've slept with a chicken if one'd offered so don't think you're anything special or even remotely permanent. You better just be wearing a condom. I don't want to have to pick up the pieces after she's gotten bored of you and sent you the way of the dodo.

She can't get pregnant! Hamish's eyebrows whipped up in alarm.

I know that, but I don't want her catching some disease because you don't want to wear a condom.

What's your problem?

Patriarchy.

I see.

Hamish began to fear Cleopatra Maria's oversized head.

Cleopatra Maria doodled number after number until Hamish left the room, convinced she was trying to come up with a formula to kill him without getting caught. He was partly right, she did want him off the face of the earth, or at least out of her *life,* and if she could have come up with a formula to accomplish this, she would have. Just like she solved the Rubic's cube without even touching it, just looked at the cube and wrote in her book, wrote and wrote until she had the cube solved, easy as pie.

Hamish finally left the room. He stood in the hall. He hopped into the kitchen for a drink of something. Anything. Just so he could forget her head.

Cleopatra Maria sat in her rocking chair and doodled in her book. How she loved her book.

Cleopatra Maria hated to admit it, but her connection to her notebook and pencil had become sexual since she gave up her short, but spectacular, sexual career. The weight and slickness of the pen. The satisfying scratching sound of the pencil lead burrowing its HB path through the fibres in the paper. The squeaks and rumbles of lead and eraser. Her book better than any lover could ever be, and no risk of pregnancy. Speaking of pregnancy.

Cleopatra Maria got up from her chair and went to the bathroom. She opened the package from the cupboard and undid her pants. She expertly aimed her pee at the wand for six seconds; a bit of urine sprinkled her fingers, the warm heat and cozy smell of her own fresh urine splashing into the toilet. Urine is sterile when it first exits the body. Sterile. Cleopatra Maria loved this thought, loved the efficiency and science of the human body even if she didn't quite believe it.

She wiped the wand with toilet paper and set it on the corner of the bath-tub. She started to sweat a little, steel bands made their way around her chest and tightened from her anxiety.

So her period was late. So what if it was late.

She was sure it was that Sunday swim last week with Oma and Tante Clotilde. She was sure she'd seen Niven scampering out of the pool. The back of his head, his skinny genius's body. This town was too small. His sperm shooting around in that water, looking for Cleopatra Maria like heat-seeking missiles.

Cleopatra Maria's tongue sticky like an earthworm gently cooking in the sun. She prayed even though she didn't believe in God, she couldn't determine His existence in her notebook, therefore He did not exist, but in moments of panic even Cleopatra Maria caught the superstitious bug.

She gave out a little scream of joy when she saw the blue line on the wand that indicated negative and the steel bands fell away.

Back in the sitting-room, Hamish gave a little jump when he heard the scream. He put down the notebook hurriedly. Couldn't make head nor tail of anything anyway.

When Frau Schnadelhuber lost her job, she chose Clotilde's bed as her place to live. Clotilde threw back the covers that morning after the Scotsman's Johnnie Walker and a million cigarettes and slid on her slap-slapping slippers that slap-slapped all the way to the door and then into the bathroom where Clotilde flushed the toilet, splashed water on her face and under her arms. Frau Schnadelhuber played at being asleep, the smell of coffee swirled into the room and still Frau Schnadelhuber played asleep. In the end, she played dead. Frau Schnadelhuber opened her eyes, not really opening her eyes because she knew what she would see, only herself unemployed, and stared through her eyelids at the ridges in the wall, the places where the seams of the paper under the white paint met. Her eyes were open but really they were closed, like cat's eyes, the inner membrane that showed the boredom, the sleepiness. She could hear the reverberating pound of her heartbeat in the drum of the mattress. Clotilde and her sister Frau Schmitt taking out plates and cutlery, swirling water in the kitchen sink, the trickling of the water through pipes, the water in Frau Schnadelhuber's blood trickling through her veins. But the water trickled slowly, trying to find the central valve system that was her heart.

Frau Schnadelhuber stayed in bed that day and the next day and the next, she stayed in bed naked under the covers but for her slip, her dress and blouse neatly folded on the straight-backed chair, the smell of boiled red cabbage simmering in the air around them.

She traded her Dirndl shell for this new, goose-down filled one, naked and vulnerable as a hermit crab, the soft grey nub that was her naked body as it transferred from shell to shell. Her new shell was softer than she was, but warmer, more secure. A wounded Siberian tiger crouched in the protective bushes, so far gone she could no longer even lick the gory wound on her breast.

Delicatessen, whispered Frau Schnadelhuber to herself. Delicatessen, the original word of love. Except her "s"'s were thick and unclean, her upper teeth fossilising in a glass by the bed.

Delicatessen, she said, and her eyelids flickered closed.

Frau Schnadelhuber agreed to sit up, but that was all she would do. She would not leave the bed under any circumstances after the Johnnie Walker night, not even to take the burning potatoes off the stove, well maybe once to take the potatoes off the stove, but not when anyone could see her.

Her toenails grew so long she could no longer put her slippers on comfortably.

Hedwig visited every day after work and smoked all brands of cigarettes in front of her mother, hoping the second-hand smoke would rouse her.

She knows you're only fake smoking, said Clotilde. She can tell from the quality of the smoke as it exits your lungs.

Well maybe she's immune, but *I* don't want to die of lung cancer.

Bloody Sapphists, said Hamish from the doorway when Clotilde bent down to straighten Frau Schnadelhuber's pillows.

I don't see why he always has to be here Oma, said Cleopatra Maria from the sitting room. Are you paying more attention to him than to me because I'm a girl? I can't help it if I wasn't born a boy.

Hannelore cringed. Hamish come here, she commanded.

Hannelore pulled him to the sitting-room and stuffed his rowdy boy-mouth full of Apfelkuchen. She made Cleopatra Maria turn off the television and eat cake with them.

It gives me zits.

You're a broomstick. I could play the piano on your ribs.

Then Hamish and Hannelore went to bed.

I hope you're protected! yelled Cleopatra Maria up the stairs, her hands on her hips. Everyone was getting sex but her.

Frau Schnadelhuber lay in Clotilde's bed, her hair streaming from her head, and decided to die. Her legs detached from her body and walked out the door, her bones crumbled among the sheets. She stuffed her head into the flowerpot on the window-sill. She had given her life to food, so she threw her intestines out the window since she wouldn't be eating ever again.

She had written up no will, but Hedwig would get everything, which was as it should be.

Now that she had nothing to do, Frau Schnadelhuber realized that her whole life had been a huge joke at her expense. Surviving two world wars, deaths and famine, the birth of her daughter, a husband from hell, and for what, for what? Simply to be told that because she had reached a certain age, she was taking up too much room, was no longer useful, no longer wanted. Her body was old, her hair grey and thinning, her skin soft and flabby where it used to be elastic and smooth, but she didn't feel old in her head until people told her she was old, hid things from her because they thought she was so old she was no longer connected with the world. On the city buses sometimes they grabbed her by the elbows and made her sit down even though once in a while she preferred to stand, to see out of the windows better. People so shocked, almost disappointed, Hedwig sometimes the worst culprit, when Frau Schnadelhuber showed some other form of life, said, I've already seen that movie, and the movie was not made in 1945, but in 1996, came out just last week at the cinema down the street.

Frau Schnadelhuber didn't feel ugly and useless until people showed her she was ugly and useless. She felt like a spider. Every leg pulled off and a dying body left to throb in the middle of the web.

Frau Schnadelhuber throbbed in the middle of the bed.

Don't go, whispered Clotilde. Don't go.

August 1996

Niagara! The Musical was scheduled to leave in a month.

New York, said Hamish. We only came here to test-drive, iron out the wrinkles. Now it's perfect, he said and patted his naked knee suggestively.

Hamish made Hannelore want to vomit and rip off her clothes all at the same time, but she was not as fast at ripping off her clothes as she once was. She didn't rip off her clothes when she was younger either, but she knew she wouldn't have had so much difficulty with her coats, bending down to pull her stockings off her toes. Hannelore ignored Hamish's hand. Ignored his hairy knee.

Well, she said.

New York, he said, and spread his legs apart even farther. His stomach hanging between his thighs like a sack of duty-free gold coins.

Well, she said. Would you like another beer?

In her head she thought about life without Hamish, how clean her sheets would be, how clean her skin would stay without the smell and sight of his grimy fingers all over her. Then Hannelore thought, The Niagara Ball.

She poured a Bitburger Pils into a glass and set it in front of him.

You and the barrel are leaving, she said.

My mascot, he said.

I could store it for you, she said.

Store it? What would I need it stored for? *Where* would you store it? This house is crammed with Kraut brick-a-brack.

You haven't ever tried to court me, said Hannelore.

Welcome to 1996, said Hamish.

This isn't how things were done when I was a girl, said Hannelore.

I don't like girls, said Hamish.

Oh, said Hannelore, and she slowly removed her stockings.

At the Auditorium, Management celebrated Ida's forced retirement. Part of the giant restructuring plan: personnel renovations to match the building renovations.

But I'm only ninety-one, whispered Ida.

Management had Ida's retirement in the works for years, and now with the new renovations and government cutbacks, her wages would go towards a new pop machine next to the coat check.

The usher-bartenders picked at free donuts and drank coffee in the staff room. A photographer from *The City Herald* was there.

But I don't want to leave, quivered Ida. She smiled bravely for the cameras, it was the city newspaper after all. Her daughter would clip out the picture for her.

"For she's a jolly good fellow," sang the younger ushers who didn't have a clue and a representative from Management, a mannequin in an expensive suit, also sang in a hearty voice while wheeling in an almond chocolate cake.

I'm allergic to nuts, whispered Ida. I'm diabetic. I didn't bring my pills.

Management's representative helped Ida into a chair and shoved a paper plate full of cake into her hands.

Ida's hair the false bright yellow of sunflowers in a hair dye box.

Hannelore felt a rolling ball of static enter her head, rest in front of her eyes so she could no longer see anything but static the colour of sunflowers, the colour of artificially flavoured cake.

Didn't you hear her say she is diabetic, said Hannelore to the ball of static, she could not bear to look at Ida, Ida working and working and working and for what? For a piece of lousy Kanadian sugar cake she couldn't eat. Ida, one of those daughters who only through sheer luck survived the war, Ida reliving name after name of her relatives murdered in the camps and trying to raise a baby daughter by herself.

And this was the way Hannelore would go too, this was how all the women would go, a piece of fancy sugar shoved into their mouths as their final reward for years and years and years of loyalty. Forget about how Hannelore suffered through the air-raids. Forget about waiting in line-ups for food, trying to make nourishing meals for her family out of *air*. Never mind standing beneath a sky full of planes, crammed full of planes, and standing on houses smashed by giant bombs. Forget how she lost most of her teeth from food shortages and malnutrition, forget moving to Kanada, learning English, finding a job, raising a son and a granddaughter because in the end all she was worth was a piece of edible plastic in the shape of a cake.

For the first time in her seventy-five years, Hannelore threw perfectly good cake in the garbage. It nearly killed her.

Hannelore & Clotilde's House: September 1996

I will buy it from you, said Hannelore. She lay fully clothed on the bed. Hamish sagged around naked and bubbling in his bearded way under the covers.

What? asked Hamish.

I want to buy it from you. I will use my entire savings.

But I don't want to sell it.

Hannelore's father clipping back the roses, roses clipped and kept up until years after he was dead they disintegrated under a carpet of aphids. Ida's hair the colour of sunflowers, her trembling hands unable to take off her name tag for the last time. Hannelore finally helped Ida unclip the tag.

I want it. I should have it. I understand what your Niagara Ball means better than you.

Maybe you just need another kiss.

I need the Ball.

Of course you're joking and I am not laughing. No, said Clotilde. No more trips. Certainly not *that* trip.

One, said Hannelore. Over Niagara Falls in a space-age barrel.

Clotilde turned the page of her newspaper. She hummed "Seemann, deine Heimat ist das Meer."

It would be nice to take a trip, said Hannelore. We haven't gone away in a long time.

Trip, muttered Clotilde. I said I would take a trip, but you can't believe how tired I am of your stupid stupid trips, I thought I made it clear that when we moved here I would never move again, never. Here I am stuck in the coldest country on Earth because *you* wanted to take a trip. Don't talk to me about trips, said Clotilde. Don't talk to me at all. *Some trip.*

Hannelore played with her fingernails for a moment. The hard nails buffed and evenly trimmed, the soft crepey skin on her hands and forearms. Hannelore ran her hands up and down her forearms, scratched her elbows. She leaned forward.

Come with me, said Hannelore.

Quatsch, said Clotilde. Go feed your bologna to someone who's hungry.

It's not Quatsch, said Hannelore. It's about not turning into stone from not moving, it's about remembering you're alive and have a future. Grabbing life by the balls and pulling until—

Clotilde pushed her glasses up her nose. Balls, said Clotilde. What balls?

You're not listening, whined Hannelore.

Clotilde picked between her bottom teeth, the only real teeth in her mouth, with her fingernail.

Sugar blown up your bottom! cried Hannelore in desperation. Mother said! Mother said! Hannelore scratched her elbows frantically, the skin on her upper arms rippling in agitation. What about

Frau Schnadelhuber? asked Hannelore. Your friend who refuses to get out of bed! Is that what will happen to us?

Ah, Frau Schnadelhuber, said Clotilde. That's why I can't leave, I have to take care of Frau Schnadelhuber. Clotilde blinked sadly behind the wall of her newspaper.

Hannelore went to the kitchen to iron her usher's skirt. Two more weeks.

How much will you pay me not to tell? said Cleopatra Maria. She rocked back and forth in her rocking chair like a metronome.

My name is Patty! she shouted to her mirror every morning. Her body a sleeping volcano. Every day she recorded the colour and size of her nipples in her notebook.

How much do you want? asked Hannelore.

Do I get my own hotel room?

You don't want to sleep with your Oma?

Will you tell me what to do all the time? Because if you do, if you tell me to do anything, I'm outta there. I want to go to bars and things. I'm of legal drinking age you know. I am twenty-six even though I'm emotionally behind.

You are a free woman, Hannelore lied. But you have to drive. You have to navigate with the map.

It would be better if you had a man to drive, said Cleopatra Maria. Men are more efficient, men are better. You said as much yourself when you wished for a grandson instead of a granddaughter.

Hannelore hung her head.

I could drive the truck, said Cleopatra Maria brightly. I have always wanted to drive a truck.

Cleopatra Maria could see herself high up off the ground, driving the truck, shifting the giant gears, running over dogs and irritating children. Cleopatra Maria had bad babysitting experiences. Babysitting the only job she could get nowadays, taking care of people's spawn, why have children if you don't want to spend time with them? She'd wiped more snotty noses and cleaned up more baby vomit than she could shake a stick at. And she liked to shake sticks sometimes. Just to see the preschoolers run.

Have you ever driven a one-ton?

A one-ton? I thought you meant a pick-up truck. When do we leave?

When does your university semester start?

There's no school this year.

Good, said Hannelore, even though she knew this probably wasn't the case. She would ask Dieter when he came back from the coffee shop with Clotilde.

Television is not what it used to be, said Cleopatra Maria and shook her head. Books these days are crap.

Hannelore guessed this was the end of the conversation. Sometimes she believed Cleopatra Maria was more Clotilde's granddaughter than her own.

Cleopatra Maria rarely saw Niven these days and she had to admit she missed him. She used to see him all the time at chess club meetings—they never spoke but they shared the same room space once a week—but then she was ousted from the club for her bad attitude.

Now I know how Captain Bligh felt, Cleopatra Maria said.

No stick-to-itiveness, Cleopatra Maria said.

What do *you* have to be bitter about? asked Hannelore. Your life is just beginning.

Try centuries of racial oppression, sighed Cleopatra Maria from her violently rocking rocking chair.

What? said Hannelore, and Hannelore let out the seam of her work-skirt one centimetre more.

Try ten years of postsecondary education and no jobs, Cleopatra Maria said. I don't have the opportunities my parents' generation had. I have nothing to live for.

What? said Hannelore.

Try the fact that I can't expect to get married and have babies, not have a job and be financially taken care of for the rest of my life. Not like you did.

Hannelore began to hum over her crossword puzzle.

I see you're still using that hairspray with the CFCs I told you not to use, called Cleopatra Maria as Hannelore hummed her way to the kitchen. Global warming, what does she care? said Cleopatra Maria and she hunkered down in her chair. The Earth turned to shit.

And no one will call me Patty when I tell them to.

Mein Schatz, is that all that's bothering you? said Hannelore and she gave Cleopatra Maria a big salad-dressing-smelling hug.

Hannelore wished Cleopatra Maria didn't feel obliged to come down to visit *every* weekend or whenever the mood hit her. Grandchildren. She loved her grandchild, but she didn't love her grandchild's attitude.

Hannelore blamed Dieter and Rosario. Such hippies, they forgot babies needed toys until Cleopatra Maria was nearly one and a half and this lack of toys distorted her mind. Hannelore sent parcels crammed with toys which Cleopatra Maria never understood. But Dieter never knew what to do with toys either, born during the war, he preferred to play with his potty, he would put it on his head and sing for hours to himself in a corner. Pretend it was a duck in the bathtub.

Hannelore blamed them for Cleopatra Maria's lack of social skills.

Where are you going, said Cleopatra Maria, bored.

Hamish came over every day for lunch, and slept Sunday and Monday nights at the house.

Why does he have to sleep over? said Cleopatra Maria. This is not a very good example you're setting for me.

Hannelore and Clotilde and Cleopatra Maria swam every Sunday morning. Clotilde came home, her hair damp, to Frau Schnadelhuber still in bed, her eyes closed, but her ears awake, playing dead, throwing herself into the role of the burden. She had no delicatessen. She had no more income. She was good for nothing but the government-run nursing home. There was no more point.

Frau Schnadelhuber lay in the bed, the star of her very own freak show: a spider with no legs, but still alive.

She managed only a few words for the press. "If it was with my dying breath" she said, "I would caution anyone against attempting the feat. I will never go over the Falls again. I would sooner walk up to the mouth of a cannon, knowing it was going to blow me to pieces than make another trip over the Falls."

—PIERRE BERTON, Niagara: A History of the Falls

Time for a trip I said, said Hannelore, her arms folded over her stomach this time.

I can't leave her here like this. No goddammit. If I go, she goes, and as you can see she's not going anywhere, said Clotilde.

She can't stay *here*, she doesn't live *here*, since when are you responsible for her?

Tell that to your pig-man wallowing in the sitting-room every weekend, said Clotilde.

Then get her up, said Hannelore. We're going on a trip. She can come or not come.

Hannelore crossed the fingers in her heart that Clotilde would come. Hannelore could not do this by herself.

No, said Clotilde.

Why don't you wash her up? said Hannelore. Wash her hair? A woman's sanity is in her hair.

I'm not going.

I'll get the shampoo, said Hannelore. I'm going to save her life.

You don't touch her, barked Clotilde.

The Royal Auditorium: October 01, 1996

Hannelore stood away from Hamish.

I have to have it, she said. You can't leave with it.

Hamish's fingers spread wide over the polished side of Anna Edson Taylor's stage-barrel, the dusky wood under his fingertips, but that other. Smell.

I have to leave, he said. It's my job. He prepared for her tears, how she would fall into his arms and they would have sex.

Yes yes you have to leave, she said, irritated. I'm just asking you to leave behind the Niagara Ball. I want to use it.

Hamish wiped his hands on his kilt. He shook his head.

A woman thing, he said softly.

His tongue slipped over "woman," and Hannelore sweated to keep her hands at her sides.

My wife also went crazy when she hit menopause, said Hamish. Loopy, he said and tapped his forehead with the finger and its split fingernail.

Left me and went to school to be a geologist, he said. Said rocks made more sense to her than men.

Hannelore struggled to keep her mouth closed. She craved his body, but was repelled in her head by all the strange wandering hairs straggling out of his nose, his ears, the hint of roses among the rotten cabbages. Bizarre male folds and thicknesses. Just because he was the only one didn't mean he had to be the only one. And right now he was standing between her and Annie.

Did I offend you? Was I too forward? I shouldn't have called you a Kraut.

Hannelore thought of him spearing his Wurst like beluga on television. The fork puncturing the skin, the pop of the skin, the juice spurting up the shiny metal of the fork. Animals going extinct.

No can do, he said. He slung his hammer back in the waist of his kilt.

How much, she said.

Not for sale. Never for sale.

Hannelore pretended not to hear. She would not beg.

Hannelore & Clotilde's House: October 02, 1996

Frau Schnadelhuber's dress and blouse neatly washed and pressed and smelling like sun, her nylons on the chair by the bed.

Clotilde washed Frau Schnadelhuber's hair in a basin. The sound of the water chuckling through her hair and Clotilde's hands in the basin. Hannelore brought in warm water and grumbled at the mess of the woman in the bed, but it wasn't *her* room, the woman wasn't her friend, and only when Clotilde was scrubbing in the shampoo did Frau Schnadelhuber unseal her nostrils for a moment. The smell of the sun. The light scent of the 4711 cologne Clotilde wore everyday and sprinkled in the bed linen.

Clotilde waved a hair-dryer over the hair, braided the hair, then kissed the tips of the braids.

I am going to the library for a few hours, said Clotilde. Don't run away, she sighed.

Frau Schnadelhuber: the body in the bed.

From the window, Hannelore watched Clotilde shuffle down the street. As soon as Hannelore saw Clotilde turn the corner, Hannelore slammed a skillet on the stove and started to fry sausage, she fried for her life, tossed in onions, rinsed Sauerkraut, spooned delicately seasoned potato salad from a styrofoam carton out onto plates. She whipped two Bitburgers from the fridge, set two beer glasses on the kitchen tray beside the plates. Remembered to put on an ashtray. Hannelore patted her bright red cheeks, picked up the tray, marched into Clotilde's bedroom.

Guten tag Frau Schnadelhuber, sang Hannelore, she smiled so hard her eyes almost disappeared in the wrinkles around her mouth and her white curls bobbed like toys.

Hannelore swept through the room, her hands full of the tray. She would have to work fast, she would have to do the job before

Clotilde got home from the library, Hannelore hammered her feet into the room and began her campaign.

Still feeling sick? asked Hannelore, You need some cheering up that's what you need.

Hannelore scooted into the hall outside the bedroom and brought in the portable turntable, opened it and immediately slammed on a record album and turned the volume up up up. Bavarian folk songs. She turned on the machine.

The orchestra set up the oom-pa-pa beat and began to slap their Lederhosen in a Bavarian frenzy.

Ahhh, Hannelore said clapping her hands, Nice nice nice.

This music was my husband's! Hannelore shouted to the room, to the stinking body in the bed. Hannelore was a little put off by what a corpse Frau Schnadelhuber seemed to have become, but she kept her surprise out of her voice and vigorously began to pour beer into glasses. She lit a cigarette, took a long drag, and set the cigarette in the ashtray.

Hannelore looked down at the body in the bed.

We have never talked, you and I Frau Schnadelhuber! We have never had a real conversation!

Hannelore bobbled her head in time to the music, she put the two plates of food on the bedside table and began to eat and drink and smoke. She patted her hands in time to the music.

Oma Hupfel had said the sausages were Frau Schnadelhuber's favourite.

Frau Schnadelhuber likes them better than cigarettes, said Oma Hupfel. And that's not nothing!

Come! Come! Hannelore said to Frau Schnadelhuber. Share with me while we talk! You're not hungry that's okay, that's okay, you can have some later. I need to ask you a favour, said Hannelore through the food in her mouth. A very big favour!

Frau Schnadelhuber lay in the bed, her mind flat like wallpaper.

I want to go on a trip, I want to go over Niagara Falls in a barrel and my friend has the perfect barrel, but suddenly he doesn't want to give it to me! What an astounding thing, nicht?

The music blared from the record, the Bavarians in its black, shiny surface bobbed their heads, slapped their thighs, swept the air with the feathers in their hats.

Clotilde and I very much appreciated that laptop computer you stole for Cleopatra Maria, did I ever tell you how much I appreciated it?

Hannelore sucked from the cigarette and took a great swallow of beer to put out the fire in her throat.

Cleopatra Maria benefited greatly from such a thing, a solid education is so so important, said Hannelore. I need you to do me a favour Frau Schnadelhuber, I need you to help me. I know you are the only one who can help me.

Hannelore turned down the music, she leaned in closely to the body's face. She took another long drag from the cigarette and deliberately blew her sausage, beer, and cigarette smoke breath into Frau Schnadelhuber's nostrils.

At first I never believed your stories about the Gestapo, or the General's Wife, or the bomb defusal. I never believed the chauffeuring, but when I saw that computer, no bag, no receipt, with my own eyes, I believed everything. Everything. I need you Frau Schnadelhuber. I need you to steal the barrel for me because you are the only one who would know how to do it. Do you hear me Frau Schnadelhuber? Can you hear me?

Frau Schnadelhuber's face had settled into a death mask, more dead than dead.

Frau Schnadelhuber? Frau Schnadelhuber, I think you have talents that you shouldn't let go to waste just because of this little job thing. I think if you stay like this, it is the same as throwing out a whole freshly roasted suckling pig. And that is a shame.

Hannelore stared at Frau Schnadelhuber.

Frau Schnadelhuber? Did you hear me? I need you to commit the Crime of the Century.

A single spark flew inside Frau Schnadelhuber's head. The Crime of the Century. Bacon fat slathered on rye bread sprinkled with salt. The Crime of the Century. The hot, sexual taste of chocolate in the mouth. The Crime of the Century.

Or perhaps Frau Schnadelhuber, said Hannelore, and her eyes narrowed to slits, so narrow she could hardly see and she put her face as close to Frau Schnadelhuber's without touching skin to skin, Hannelore's voice soft, almost sweet: Maybe Frau Schnadelhuber, you are just a liar, you are a liar, and I was wrong to believe you, I look at you here in hogging up my sister's bed, breaking her heart, and I really can't believe you were a spy for the Resistance, I think you are, and have always been, just an unemployed waitress, *and* a burden, *and* insignificant. Because no spy would give up like you have, no one who lived through the war, period, would give up like you have.

Hannelore took another bite of sausage, a swallow of beer, ducked her head and hissed into Frau Schnadelhuber's face: When my husband was killed and I had no food to give to my son, did I feel sorry for myself and just lie down and die? You were there, is that what you did? I don't believe anything you said, you are a fraud, you made it all up! *You made it all up*!

Hannelore did not see the spit that shot from Frau Schnadelhuber's mouth, the spit was so fast, so precise and deadly in its aim, the projectile spit that hit like a watery bullet and threw Hannelore's head back several centimetres with its force.

I will rent a truck for a day, big enough to hold the barrel, whispered Hannelore through the spit running down her face. You said you used to drive, you can drive it, and you can help me steal the barrel.

Drive? Frau Schnadelhuber's voice scratched the air.

And steal, said Hannelore.

Steal? Frau Schnadelhuber's voice flew like a rusty tin bird.

The electricity inside Frau Schnadelhuber churned so hard it burst the surface and, suddenly, her bones sat up in the bed.

Frau Schnadelhuber loved to drive.

Frau Schnadelhuber remembered back in the war, working as a chauffeur for the General's Wife.

Driving you see many things, said Frau Schnadelhuber to Clotilde one afternoon in the library, I was a *beautiful* driver, learned in the war when so many men went off. Chauffeured a General's Wife. Like any servant, see everything, tell nothing. If you choose to keep your job. Act like the walls. Be the mattresses in hotel rooms. The General's Wife died of a heart attack in an air-raid. Not the fear of bombs that killed her, but the fear of living and then being caught by the Gestapo.

Quatsch! said Clotilde.

You listen, said Frau Schnadelhuber. Better a heart attack than if the police had caught her, I'm sure the attack was fake, a drug to commit suicide, the timing was so perfect. She used her husband the General as a way of accessing the information. People talk about resistance, now she resisted, passed on plans for the resistance, the layout of a camp. I ended up in a work camp, charged for a "defeatist" attitude, I was lucky as hell. Lucky as hell. I need a cigarette.

Could you drive a one-ton truck? Hannelore asked the body sitting up in the bed, the face with the eyes rolling spastically under the lids.

Could Frau Schnadelhuber drive a one-ton, what a question, Frau Schnadelhuber could drive anything on wheels, drove a tank once, drove her little taxi around the heaps of rubble that used to be her town before the petrol ran out. Drove ambulances, her magic wand the gear shift.

I need a cigarette, croaked Frau Schnadelhuber. She opened her eyes.

Hannelore clapped her greasy sausage hands over her mouth and began to cry—hot, thick tears transformed her head into a giant hard-boiled egg.

Of course I'll get you a cigarette! and Hannelore crackled the plastic frantically around the stale package of abandoned cigarettes, stuck another one in her mouth, this celebratory smoke between enemies suddenly turned allies.

So, on that cold, windswept afternoon of October 24, 1901, while realizing she would have to get into more utilitarian clothing, she refused to put on a short skirt in Niagara Falls, New York, because "it would be unbecoming a woman of refinement and my years."

She wore a large hat, a long black dress with a tightly corseted waist and puff sleeves when she entered a rowboat to Grass Island, above the Falls. On the island, she sent her two oarsmen into the bushes while she went to the other end of the island to change into a short skirt and take off her black stockings and hat.

—PERCY ROWE, Niagara Falls & Falls

Hannelore, Frau Schnadelhuber, Clotilde, and Cleopatra Maria sat around the table in the sitting-room. They looked as though they were playing canasta, but this was no regular game of canasta because they played with the cards that had been dealt them the day they were born.

Hannelore described the Niagara Ball, the tunnels where Hamish kept the ball.

Frau Schnadelhuber listened, her brain busier than a food processor.

Cleopatra Maria couldn't wait to be old, she wanted to be old so that her life could also be this exciting. She held her mechanical pencil above the graph paper like she wanted to stab the paper and as Hannelore spoke, she drew on the paper, her pencil dipping like the head of a loon and coming up with fish after fish.

Once, Clotilde banged the table with her fist and shouted, Impossible! I'm not participating in this nonsense!

Cleopatra Maria's pencil bounced and the tip of the lead crumbled.

Frau Schnadelhuber winked and Hannelore took out her breasts and pointed them at Clotilde.

Clotilde said, All right, we could do it that way.

Cleopatra Maria clicked more lead out of her pencil.

The Royal Auditorium: October 03, 1996

Hannelore, Frau Schnadelhuber, Cleopatra Maria and Clotilde
slinked through the tunnels under the Royal Auditorium. Hannelore
guided them past stacks of chairs, metal boxes of lighting equipment
never used. Dress mannequins with antique dimensions, purple
satin panties an understudy from the last show forgot to collect
after her rendezvous with a janitor. Coiled cables, piles of mouse turd.
Black beetles. A mannequin dressed like a Royal Auditorium usher.

Ida! said Hannelore.

Ida scuttled behind a stack of chairs.

Ida come out, what's the problem, why you hiding down here?
asked Hannelore.

I forgot, Ida said. I came to work ready for my shift and then I
remembered Management fired me.

Bastards! said Frau Schnadelhuber. But this is good. We can use
another body.

We can't use Ida! said Hannelore.

Can't use me for what? asked Ida.

Nothing, said Hannelore.

The Crime of the Century, said Frau Schnadelhuber.

Oma wants to steal Hamish's Niagara Ball, said Cleopatra Maria.
I have been coerced into helping them.

Here it is, said Hannelore, but I don't know where he is. He is
always around it, always.

Jesus Christ it's an ugly colour, said Cleopatra Maria. It makes
me want to throw up. And it's not a ball, it's an egg! You're going over
Niagara Falls in this thing? Forget it! I'm telling Mummy and Daddy!

What are you doing? said Ida.

It's all in the attitude, said Frau Schnadelhuber. Just act as
though it belongs to you.

It does belong to me, said Hannelore.

There you go, said Clotilde.

We could never move this, said Cleopatra Maria.

Hannelore leaned against the Niagara Ball and slowly it began to roll.

Hey! said Cleopatra Maria. Cleopatra Maria poked the Ball from behind and in front. She kicked the side. She tried to stab it with her mechanical pencil and failed. She pulled out her tape measure and measured the diameter and the length of the ball and recorded the numbers in her notebook.

Open it, she commanded.

We have to go now! said Hannelore.

Open it now or I'm not helping! I don't want an omelette for an Oma! I have a responsibility, said Cleopatra Maria.

Hannelore slid open the trap door and Cleopatra Maria jumped into the ball. The ball quivered. Solar calculators suck, said Cleopatra Maria from inside the ball.

There's a light, said Hannelore.

Found it!

Cleopatra Maria punched numbers into the calculator, consulted the numbers she'd previously recorded after finding them on the Internet displaying the height of the Falls, the amount of water going over the Falls in summer, fall, and winter, the depth and force of the water at the bottom of the Falls. Her pencil scratched her paper busily. The Ball wobbled from the force of her brain.

Impressive, Cleopatra Maria said, and stepped out of the Ball. I am impressed. No more dangerous than jumping off a wall that's half a metre high. I like it!

That's a relief! said Clotilde.

Hannelore slid the trap door shut. The women began to roll the Niagara Ball in the direction of the stage door.

No, said Hannelore, we can't do this during the daylight, people will see us, everyone will know.

Hannelore began to sweat.

Attitude! shouted Frau Schnadelhuber.

Attitude, they all whispered.

But why are you going through the stage door? said Ida.

To get it out of the building without being seen.

You don't have to go through the stage door. There's a door leading to the outside on the west side.

But I have never seen this door, said Hannelore. I've worked here for years and never heard of this door.

Ida shone the flashlight she'd forgotten to return along with her uniform into the mannequins. She began to push them aside.

The door is an old door, before renovations, whispered Ida.

Cleopatra Maria shone a flashlight on her plans while everyone else wrestled slowly with the mannequins blocking the alternate tunnel. She took out her pencil and drew in a door.

Ida disappeared ahead past the mannequins, shining the usher's flashlight on the floor, ahead of her orthopaedic shoes. Ida walked behind the light through the tunnels and Hannelore dabbed at the sweat on her forehead.

You, said Frau Schnadelhuber. You Frau Schmitt, go wait in the truck. You are emitting bad vibrations, I can smell how bad your attitude is and I don't want someone smelling you and following us. Ida knows the way, you go wait in the truck.

Hannelore dabbed her forehead. She opened her blouse, dabbed at her armpits with a Kleenex and stumbled back the other way.

Ida showed them the door and they rolled the Niagara Ball across the parking lot to the truck like the Ball was a baby carriage full of empty, fully-refundable bottles. Cleopatra Maria raised the back door of the truck, let down a ramp and they rolled the Ball up.

There, said Frau Schnadelhuber.

There, said Clotilde.

There, said Cleopatra Maria.

Can I come? said Ida.

Edmonton, Canada: October 03, 1996

For the trip to Niagara Falls, Hannelore would rent a one-ton truck, and Cleopatra Maria would drive Frau Schnadelhuber's station wagon. But they needed to store the Niagara Ball for the time being until Hannelore's vacation time began.

You didn't think of the storage problem before we stole the Ball? asked Frau Schnadelhuber, her hands on her hips.

We could put it in the back yard, said Clotilde.

Teenagers might steal it, said Hannelore. The police might see it if Hamish decides to hunt for it.

We have no room, we have no room, fretted Hannelore by herself in the front hall while the Ball waited in the rented truck, time and money ticking by.

Oh Oma, sighed Cleopatra Maria. She walked up the stairs to the kitchen for a glass of prune juice.

All the rooms in the townhouse were full of angular, wedding-gift furniture. The steep, narrow staircase that went up the centre of the house took up more room. The basement crammed with shelves of preserves and old bottles of Sekt turned sour from old age in 1989. Gardening tools, Dieter and Rosario's hippie furniture, and Cleopatra Maria's bicycle she never rode because the bicycle company used sweat shops.

You don't expect me to *throw* out the bicycle! said Hannelore.

Throwing out would be too good for it, said Cleopatra Maria from her rocking chair.

Hannelore shuddered at the waste.

Hannelore went upstairs to the kitchen and watched Cleopatra Maria sip thick prune juice through a see-through curly straw.

I have so many things, Hannelore said to Cleopatra Maria. Think! Where can we put the Niagara Ball?

Cleopatra Maria slurped.

I don't need all these things, said Hannelore, and she banged out the kitchen door to the sitting-room, the most crammed room of all. Hannelore circled the room, around the table, the television set, the sofa, Cleopatra Maria's rocking chair.

Cleopatra Maria wandered into the sitting-room and plopped herself down in the rocking chair with her glass of juice, the straw still in her mouth.

Why do people keep giving me all these *things*, muttered Hannelore. Where can I put the Ball with all these things in the way? Where will all these things go when I'm gone? I must make room. Here, Cleopatra Maria, take these crystal glasses. Take them for when you get married. Have this silver nutcracker set.

Hannelore dumped a box in Cleopatra Maria's lap.

Can I have the silverware instead? said Cleopatra Maria.

What are we supposed to eat with?

Oma, what am I supposed to drink out of crystal liqueur glasses? Coca-Cola? You know I disapprove of the regular consumption of alcohol. I'm not like you guys, drinking all the time for medicinal purposes. When I drink, I drink to get drunk and I don't need fancy glasses to do it.

But what about your guests? asked Hannelore. You don't expect your guests to drink out of the same bottle you drank out of?

Cleopatra Maria stared straight ahead. She would not even acknowledge such a colossally stupid question.

Hannelore scratched her elbows, ran her hands up and down her forearms.

I have no room, I have no room, I have no room. Clotilde! Frau Schnadelhuber! *There is no room.*

Put it in the backyard I said, said Clotilde.

What if it rains? said Hannelore

It's not waterproof? You're riding in it over a waterfall and it's not waterproof?

198

Hannelore stopped her scratching for a moment.

I don't want it dirty, said Hannelore.

Well then, said Cleopatra Maria from her rocking chair. I guess you have to give it back. That's a relief.

Frau Schnadelhuber bounced into the doorway. Let's go, she said.

The Delicatessen: October 04, 1996: Midnight

The Ball sat in the delicatessen. Floated in the delicatessen. They stood around it in a circle and looked.

Cleopatra Maria had never been in a shopping mall at night. She felt like a vampire.

This is all very exciting, said Oma Hupfel. A giant orange egg. What is it and what are you going to do with it? Is it a space ship?

Everyone will see it, said Cleopatra Maria. This is ridiculous.

Attitude, said Frau Schnadelhuber.

Whatever this egg is, I don't like the colour, said Oma Hupfel. Gaudy.

Oma Hupfel bustled into the backroom and brought out a step-ladder.

Oma Hupfel carefully draped a yellow tablecloth over the top. Then a smaller tablecloth with pansies embroidered on the edges on top of the yellow tablecloth.

I still don't like it, said Oma Hupfel. But at least it's dressed.

Oma Hupfel wiped her hands on her apron. The tablecloths look good, she said. Don't you think they look good? Those are nice colours together, purple and yellow.

Put a wreath of dried flowers on top, said Frau Schnadelhuber. That will make it better.

Oma Hupfel was bored working with teenagers now that the other older waitresses and cooks were all eliminated by fax. Oma Hupfel was the chief of too many young people, young people were so unreliable, but for six dollars an hour, who cared about being reliable? They weren't paid enough to be reliable. Six dollars wasn't enough to make anyone under sixty-five care about anything.

I'm sure the Madame would disapprove, said Oma Hupfel

absent-mindedly, her mind absent. She tweaked the corner of the yellow tablecloth straighter.

But those youngsters, Oma Hupfel said, they won't notice anything. They're not paid enough to notice, just hack at the salamis, undercook the potatoes, weigh their mail on the meat scale. Talk to their boyfriends instead of scrubbing the baseboards. Not like the old days.

Oma Hupfel rolled a salami in her hands, the meat cutter in her head shaving and slicing.

What about the customers? asked Clotilde.

As long as they get their food on time and hot, they won't see it, said Frau Schnadelhuber. It will be safe here for the rest of the week, and then we can take it.

What is it? asked Oma Hupfel.

I'm going to ride over Niagara Falls in it, said Hannelore.

Holy Jesus! said Oma Hupfel, and she clasped her apron to her bosom. You will be killed!

Cleopatra Maria quietly put her arm in the glass-fronted fridge and pulled a chunk of sugary apple from the inside of a long, uncut apple Strudel. Oma Hupfel swivelled her head and looked at Cleopatra Maria for a moment, the cold, cooked apple in Cleopatra Maria's mouth, Cleopatra Maria's fingers covered in sticky flakes of Strudel pastry. Oma Hupfel turned her head back to Hannelore.

Can I come too? asked Oma Hupfel.

Hannelore grunted.

She felt no impact when the barrel struck the water; she simply knew it had dropped below the surface. No sound reached her. She felt alone, forsaken. About a minute passed and then she felt the barrel starting upward. It shot out of the water ten or fifteen feet into the air, dropped and plunged again, and was hurled back into the cavern behind the sheet of water. There it was picked up by the force of the waves, dashed around in mid-air and dropped onto the rocks. She could feel herself being whirled about and lifted like "butter in a churn."

—PIERRE BERTON, Niagara: A History of the Falls

Trans-Canada Highway: Thursday, October 17, 1996: 8:16 A.M.

Once they are on the road, Cleopatra Maria and her Oma sit in the car and the only one who talks is the car engine. They cannot sing together. They don't know any of the same songs. Both Cleopatra Maria and Hannelore long for the buffer zone of food or the television to show them how to be grandmother and granddaughter. Cleopatra Maria longs for a normal grandmother who is asexual and who would make Cleopatra Maria the centre of her life. Hannelore longs for a great-grandson from a granddaughter whom she wishes were asexual. Cleopatra Maria drives along the highway, and she looks often into the rearview mirror at the truck behind them, the women in the front seat who keep kissing each other at stoplights.

They can't do that on the highway, says Cleopatra Maria. I should get out at the next light and tell them to cut it out. They're a potential traffic menace.

What? says her grandmother. Stop who from doing what?

Nothing, says Cleopatra Maria.

Nothing, says her grandmother. Always you say "nothing."

All right, says Cleopatra Maria. Tante Clotilde and Frau Schnadelhuber keep kissing at the stoplights, they're necking in the truck and one of these stops they're not going to see us and they're going to get lost.

What a beautiful landscape, says Hannelore. Look at all the cows. Kanadians take such good care of the land, and that makes it nice to get out of the city, nicht?

Cleopatra Maria drives along the highway, she looks often at the rearview mirror. Cleopatra Maria full to the gills with Birth Control Pills and her suitcase spilling extra packages just in case. Now if she were an eighty-five-year-old lesbian like Tante Clotilde she wouldn't have to worry about getting pregnant. And she worries about her Oma sometimes and that pig-dog Hamish. They probably don't use condoms, Hamish looks like the type who would complain about how condoms dull the sensitivity of his precious penis, and what if there was a fluke? What if there is still a fertile egg floating around in her Oma and one of Hamish's stupid sperm finds it? There are always *flukes*, Cleopatra Maria hates flukes and only after many years of trial and error has she realized that the world cannot be purely translated with her mechanical pencil into her notebook without the consideration of flukes—the fly in the ointment, the hair in her otherwise delicious soup. This whole trip inspired by a fluke.

As if Annie Edson Taylor survived going over the Falls in a crappy little barrel for any reason other than a fluke. But of course her Oma and Tante Clotilde and Frau Schnadelhuber will be all right. Hamish may be a pig-dog, but that doesn't mean he's stupid. Cleopatra Maria has been in the vessel itself, thrown herself against the hard walls inside, banged it with a sledge-hammer at the seams, hammered at the elaborate bolt that holds the trap-door closed. She has calculated the surface area of the vessel, the potential angles at which the vessel will jump over the Falls, the vessel's impact at the bottom while filled with three women weighing in at 165, 100, and 140 pounds if Frau Schnadelhuber goes in too, 405 pounds total. She is not so sure about the force of the water though. And the possiblity of *fluke*. Cleopatra Maria believes she has accounted for all the fluke possibilities, but what if there was one she missed? She suggested to her Oma that the three women fast and abstain from sex for a week before doing the trip and her Oma gave Cleopatra Maria a hairy eyeball so hairy Cleopatra Maria felt her sinuses flood with allergy-induced mucous.

Cleopatra Maria looks in the rear-view mirror. Frau Schnadelhuber has her hand on one of Tante Clotilde's breasts.

All that sex can't be good for old people—Cleopatra Maria used to believe that old people just kissed and hugged when they got into bed together—but Cleopatra Maria has accidentally walked into rooms full of sweaty and sexy old relatives too many times to count. She wonders how their hearts can stand it. Must be the Heart Pills they're always taking. Cleopatra Maria can't wait until she turns eighty-five. Then she can do whatever the hell she wants.

How did you meet Opa? asks Cleopatra Maria suddenly.

In a hiking group, says Hannelore fondly. A Christian hiking group.

I don't know what's so romantic about hiking. Sweating and bugs.

There was no such thing as sweating and bugs in those days, says Hannelore.

———

Frau Schnadelhuber drives the one-ton. Her body suddenly fresh and full after such a long time of bed-rest, maybe just lying in bed for a little while was what she needed all along. She and Clotilde listen to rock and roll on the radio. Frau Schnadelhuber is sure she was born forty years too early, she would have loved to have been a rock star. Negro music they used to call it, she loved the Negro music so much. Louis Armstrong, a fine fine musician. Then later Jimi Hendrix. Even now the music on the truck radio, not familiar, makes her tap her foot with a rhythm that is distinctly like she and Clotilde doing what they do under the dark and delicious weight of the goose-down duvet. They move to a rock and roll song only they can hear. Frau Schnadelhuber is addicted to Clotilde, like cigarettes, like gorgonzola. Gorgonzola the most delicious thing on this intensely troubled Earth and life without gorgonzola would be the same as death. Like breathing, like loving. Frau Schnadelhuber is in love and it has nothing to do with her but her body's overwhelming needs, the pain only Clotilde can soothe with her voice, deep like fresh tobacco.

Are you sure you've never smoked? rumbles Frau Schnadelhuber.

Smoked? Please, says Clotilde. We were too poor to waste money on cigarettes.

You could get most things through the back door if you were smart, says Frau Schnadelhuber.

Clotilde and Frau Schnadelhuber's bodies like rock and roll.

The rumble of the truck's engine makes Frau Schnadelhuber moist between the between. She reaches for Clotilde.

Oh you, says Clotilde.

———

I've never been to Niagara Falls before, says Cleopatra Maria.

Yes, when you were a baby, says Hannelore.

When I was a baby, when I was a baby, the most exciting things I did were when I was a baby. Now I do nothing. I play with my computer and watch tv and strangers give me degrees because I'm supposedly so smart, but really I'm just bored and have no life.

You should go out more, agrees Hannelore. Get a boyfriend.

Cleopatra Maria accidentally jams her elbows into the horn. The station wagon swerves onto the shoulder of the road.

Sorry! she shouts to the road. The Saskatchewan dust around the car.

I thought you were a better driver than this, says Hannelore.

You provoked me. You should never provoke a driver when she's driving.

They are still behind us, says Hannelore. Good.

———

Maybe we don't talk enough, says Clotilde. Maybe we have too much sex. We talk too much about the past and we talk too much about sex.

Too much sex, thinks Frau Schnadelhuber. Is such a thing possible? She went for sixty years without sex. Could she ever have too much sex?

What do you want to talk about? asks Frau Schnadelhuber.

Well. How are you feeling. Now that you're well again.

Good. Good. I feel much better. And you?

Good.

They drive on. The new car smell in the cab of the truck. Clotilde runs her hand over the dashboard. Runs a Kleenex from her purse over the dashboard.

Dusty, she says.

Yes.

Next stop we should buy some cleaner. Clean the inside of this truck.

Good idea. Next time—no.

What? says Clotilde.

Next time I will try to make you have three orgasms in a row. I brought along extra lubricator.

Good idea, says Clotilde. After we clean the inside of the truck.

Of course!

Of course.

————

Daddy and Mummy wouldn't approve, says Cleopatra Maria. She sucks from a box of juice. Peach and orange juice that slops in her stomach.

Your Daddy and Mummy don't understand, says Hannelore.

I don't understand, says Cleopatra Maria. And I don't understand why you hang around that Hamish. He's a lazy jerk. Daddy and Mummy wouldn't like that either.

A "yerk"? says Hannelore. What is a "yerk"?

Oh forget it, says Cleopatra Maria. You always play deaf when you don't like what I'm saying.

What a rotten mouth, thinks Hannelore. Can she help it if Cleopatra Maria mumbles? Hannelore rolls down the window a sliver. Closes it when the wind ruffles her hair and blows cold air and dust in her face. Hannelore takes a sip of her apple juice. Smacks her lips. Apple juice sifted and processed until it tastes more like water than water. Soon she will have to pee. Cleopatra Maria will make a fuss.

Not agaaaain, she'll say.

What did you say? says Cleopatra Maria.

Hmm?

I heard you imitating me in your head. I can read minds when I feel like it you know. I just use the other ninety percent of my brain.

What a beautiful day for a drive, says Hannelore, and she sucks up the last of her apple juice. She has to admit Kanadian apple juice quenches the thirst better than the thick and cloudy apple juice in Germany. Everything in Kanada simply wonderful, including the apple juice. Hannelore crosses her hands in her lap.

————

My history book doesn't say anything about plain Christian hiking groups during the war, says Cleopatra Maria. The books say you had to belong to one of those Hitler Jugend groups if you were a certain age or you wouldn't get ahead in school.

It was a Christian hiking group. Not Hitler Jugend.

So you were in one of those Hitler youth groups, says Cleopatra Maria.

Hitler group? says Hannelore. It was a Christian group.

But you were the right age.

The hiking group was not politically affiliated, says Hannelore, her mouth stiff.

You were one of those girls. One of those Hitler Youth girls.

When I was younger I was part of the Bund deutscher Mädel, yes. You had to be.

Oh my god. Was Opa a Hitler youth?

Oh there's a rest stop. Stop. Stop there.

Where?

There, the sign.

That's not for another two kilometres.

Hannelore suddenly remembers what she and the other girls had to wear for sports. White tops with the rhombus on the chest and the Hakenkreuz in the middle of the rhombus. Clotilde was too old to be part of the Bund deutscher Mädel.

If you had a boyfriend, says Hannelore, he could do the driving and I could be a great-grandmother. Two birds with one rock.

The station wagon swerves violently.

———

Your great-niece is driving like a fool, says Frau Schnadelhuber. All over the road.

Clotilde's eyelids jolt awake.

She is distracted, says Clotilde thickly. She never gets any sex. It has infected her brain.

But every time I look at her she is eating a Birth Control Pill.

Her womb terrifies her.

Poor girl.

Farmers' fields whirr by.

What is the secret to a long-lasting relationship, says Clotilde.

Do you mean good or lasting, because I was in a lasting relationship and it was never good.

I mean good *and* lasting, says Clotilde. You are my longest. We have been together almost ten years. You are a miracle.

Clean regularly in the armpits, clean regularly between the legs, says Frau Schnadelhuber.

That makes sense, says Clotilde. But not too much. You don't want to wash away your smell. Cleopatra Maria is always washing, always shaving away her smell, that's why there is never any boyfriend over for the weekend. And she is too skinny.

Maybe we should tell her, says Frau Schnadelhuber.

Yes, and she would make our lives miserable forever.

The cab stinks of disinfectant. Clotilde slurps from her box of juice.

Soon Clotilde will have to pee.

———

Maybe Niagara Falls is overrated, says Frau Schnadelhuber. A tourist trap. I have seen pictures full of nothing but neon lights.

You don't know what you're talking about. Niagara Falls are magnificent.

Your sister has never liked me.

Really she doesn't like anyone.

Why not?

She's not happy unless she has something to complain about. Her husband made her very happy because he never listened to her. Hamish made her happy because he was always making a mess. You being with me makes her happy even though she hates it. It gives her brains something to do.

I see, says Frau Schnadelhuber. So she needs me.

Exactly correct, says Clotilde. Look, dead deer.

Oh what a shame, says Frau Schnadelhuber. Such beautiful, graceful animals.

———

Dead deer, says Cleopatra Maria.

Where?

Back there, you missed it.

Tsk tsk. That would never happen on the Autobahn.

Just like there never used to be sweating and bugs?

I do not remember sweating and bugs, therefore there never used to be sweating and bugs.

The reason that would never happen on the Autobahn, says Cleopatra Maria, is because all the deer have been shot and their heads stuck up in restaurants.

Cleopatra Maria remembers the last time she visited Germany. Being forced to eat venison ragout under twelve giant stuffed deer heads all in a row. But I'm a vegetarian! she shouted.

Eat the rest of my Spargel, said Rosario.

It was asparagus season.

There's too much cholesterol in the sauce on the Spargel! shouted Cleopatra Maria.

Dieter sliced his Frikadelle in disgust and stuffed a piece in his mouth. I need more beer, he said. Good Spargel, he said as he bit into a giant white asparagus tip.

You're too skinny, said Hannelore, and she put another spoonful of her own venison ragout onto Cleopatra Maria's plate.

Cleopatra Maria screamed and all the deer heads on the walls of the restaurant began to cry giant deer tears.

That's not true, says Hannelore. All the deer in Germany have not been decapitated.

When are you going to call Daddy and Mummy, says Cleopatra Maria. She rolls down her window and sticks her elbow out into the rushing air.

Later. At the first hotel.

So the story is you're taking me on a trip so we'll get to know each other better right?

Right, says Hannelore.

That's so Walt Disney. We spend every weekend together anyway. Don't forget to call them.

I won't forget.

You'll forget. Maybe I should do it.

I'll remember. That wind is messing my hair.

I hope I live to be one hundred and five, says Cleopatra Maria suddenly.

The inside of the car reeks of disinfectant. The rearview mirror sparkles.

Time to eat, Hannelore says.

We ate an hour aaaago!

Hannelore reinserts her bobby pins, pats her hair. Time to eat, she says.

Cleopatra Maria flicks on the blinker, pulls the station wagon off to the right.

By the time we get there I'll be forty-five years old, Cleopatra Maria grumbles.

I remember when I was forty-five years old.

I don't want to hear it, says Cleopatra Maria.

Hannelore decides they will stay the night. Wherever they are.

213

Maple Creek, Saskatchewan, says Cleopatra Maria. Butt-hole of the universe.

———

Cleopatra Maria puts all the Maple Creek motel soaps in the pockets of her anorak. In the motel liquor store she tries to choose between what kind of rum she would like in her Coke. She's never made her own rum and Coke before, just asked for it and they gave it to her. White rum? Dark rum? Maybe she would like rum and 7-Up. Why isn't there a drink called rum and 7-Up? She will buy a bottle of 7-Up just in case. She will sneak rum into her three-litre bottle of 7-Up and quietly get blasted in the motel room while her Oma watches the television. Both Cleopatra Maria and her Oma will try to ignore the rhythmic banging of the bed in the adjoining room where Frau Schnadelhuber and Tante Clotilde go at it.
Cleopatra Maria paces back and forth in front of the wall of rums.

Would you like to try some Baby Canadian Champagne?

Cleopatra Maria takes a sip from the sample plastic cup of champagne offered by the old woman at the taste-testing booth in the liquor store. The woman has a face that looks like pudding. Hair the colour of mud, and very very dirty fingernails. The woman reminds Cleopatra Maria of earthworms.

I'll take two bottles of *that*, says Cleopatra Maria, her tongue celebrating the taste of the fizzy alcohol.

Remember, says the woman, drink and drive.

Yeah, yeah, says Cleopatra Maria. She carries the bottles in her bag under her arm to the station wagon. She pours out the giant bottle of 7-Up into the dust in the parking lot. Watches the volcanic pop fizz in the dirt. Slowly pours one bottle of Baby Canadian Champagne into the emptied 7-Up bottle, puts the other bottle of champagne in the trunk of the station wagon.

What are you drinking from that bottle there? says Hannelore back in the motel room.

7-Up, says Cleopatra Maria. You want some?

Too sweet, says Hannelore.

———

Of course I will jump over Niagara Falls too, says Frau Schnadel-huber.

You will? says Clotilde.

I have nothing left to live for without my job, without you. What difference would it make if I lived or died?

We're not going to die, frowns Clotilde. The vessel is proven one hundred percent effective.

Who says?

You saw Cleopatra Maria do the physics. If I could I would buy you your job back, says Clotilde grandly. I would buy the delicatessen for you if I could. I am so tired of Hannelore's trips. But she needs me to take care of her.

———

Cleopatra Maria's tongue so thick in her head from champagne she's sure she swallowed a Gila Monster. In her head, she runs through the conjugation of the verb "to drink" in Latin: bibo, I drink, bibis, you drink, bibit, he/she/it drinks, bibimus— Cleopatra Maria belches.

She puts her hand over her mouth and giggles in the dark.

———

They drive slowly through Saskatchewan. Sleet turns the prairies to mud, dribbles down and fogs up the windshields. The station wagon and one-ton drive over tar and pockets of mud on the detour roads, mud pulls and sucks at the tires, splashes the windshields. Cleopatra Maria begins to get sad about this whole thing, this whole trip, this stupid idea of her Oma's. Cleopatra Maria also remembers that alcohol is a depressant, so of course she feels terrible, of course she wants to weep, of course the mud seems to oppress her, of course her hands shake from a slight hangover on the steering wheel and she wants to turn the car around and go home. Cleopatra Maria is twenty-six years old, she should know better, she shouldn't have played along in the deception, her parents will kill her. And why would anyone want to go over Niagara Falls in a barrel anyway?

The slip-slip of the windshield wipers; the muddy fields and the muddy overcast sky melt into each other.

Cleopatra Maria admits that she is mostly along only for the ride and because she wanted to get away from her parents. She didn't think of what she was actually *doing*. She didn't think of what her Oma was actually proposing. Why this plan is happening. Cleopatra Maria decides to read her Oma's mind.

She prods her Oma's brain, travels the whorls and bumps of her grandmother's brain with her mental fingers like Braille. Glides in the valleys, over the slick layer of grey matter. Cleopatra Maria first off sees Niagara Falls of course, the water silent—sensual and slow like oil. Niagara Falls on the brain. Cleopatra Maria hears Hannelore's empty house in Germany, the sound of Hannelore's feet clumping up the stairs to the bedroom with the empty twin beds. Sees Hannelore's work shoes on the carpet of the Royal Auditorium, the comfortably stretched and smelly black leather. A plate of freshly cooked white Spargel covered with yellow sauce. A frosty crystal jigger glass full of Kirschwasser. She hears an air-raid siren and watches an American tank ramming through the garden hedge. Sees a very healthy bowel movement and feels proud of the good quality of the stools. Tours an opera diva's chaotic dressing room. Sees more twin beds. Sees an erect penis emerging from under a kilt—

Cleopatra Maria shuts down transmission. This is the problem with reading minds. The whorls all point in the same sex direction. Getting it, not getting it, hating it, longing for it, resenting it, forgetting it, doing it, complaining about it. Cleopatra Maria remains disgusted with the one-track mindedness of the people around her.

Yes Cleopatra Maria wants to have sex; if Niven could have controlled himself, she may have even had had sex with him by now. But only so she could say she did it and stop being abnormal. Stop obsessing about it and get on with her life. Poor, sweet, premature-ejaculating Niven. Cleopatra Maria saw him two weeks ago at the university in the graduate students' lounge sitting at one of the tables looking confusedly at the submarine sandwich in his hands. She knew he wasn't sure which end of the sandwich to start eating—that was always his submarine sandwich dilemma and the dilemma usually lasted for a good four minutes unless she was there to point out which end of the sandwich he should bite first. Cleopatra Maria looked at poor Niven, felt so sorry for him and his sandwich, wanted to risk his ejaculating and speak to him when she suddenly saw the picture behind him. A picture of Athena, the goddess of wisdom. The smartest, meanest professional virgin ever, bursting out of her father's skull dressed in full armour. In her quest for role models, Cleopatra Maria decided that Athena made a lot of sense. Cleopatra Maria would like to burst out of someone's skull in full armour. Abstain from sex, lose her thoughts about sex completely and concentrate on sharpening her brain even more. Then she could forget about pumping her body full of Pills and do something useful with her time. Stop thinking about Niven—that premature-ejaculating idiot—and finally discover the cure for cancer.

I love you Oma, says Cleopatra Maria suddenly.

What?

I love you!

Oh I love you too mein Schatz, and Hannelore gives Cleopatra Maria a happy fruit-juice breath pat on the arm.

———

Hannelore wonders if she misses Hamish. She does not believe she misses Hamish. She has barely thought about him since she hugged him goodbye forever. He could cry on command he told her later, he said he got into her pants by pretending to cry and it worked because she was sentimental.

Nothing better than turning on the waterworks to butter up the ladies, he said.

She was furious that he manipulated her. Also she hardly ever wears slacks so how could he say he got into her pants?

That means seduce, he said. Getting into someone's pants means to seduce them.

Another stupid American expression. But he would have been more furious if he'd known how she slept with him only because of the Niagara Ball. Well mostly only because of the Niagara Ball. Maybe he's guessed it.

She thinks not.

———

They follow the Trans-Canada highway signs, stop over in motels in Swift Current, Moose Jaw, and Virden when the rain and mud get too depressing, or their bums too sore, or their bladders too full, or their mouths too cranky. In the motel room in Virden, Manitoba, Cleopatra Maria traces the map with her mechanical pencil. Her brain pulses from the excitement of navigation.

What navigation? says Frau Schnadelhuber. We just have to follow the signs and stay on the same road the whole way.

Cleopatra Maria charts the trip on a graph in her notebook. Hours between rest stops, gas, food consumption, the number of toilet breaks.

Now see, Oma, if we didn't stop so many times, if we peed in buckets in the car instead of stopping at every rest area we come to and just threw the pee out the window while we're driving, things would go much faster, says Cleopatra Maria.

That is a wonderful idea mein Schatz, says Hannelore. Hannelore stares at the instructions on the coffee machine set up between her and Cleopatra Maria's twin beds. She opens a bag of the ground coffee, sniffs the coffee.

Hannelore makes another cup of coffee. Eats another sticky butter tart from the gas station food store. Peeing in buckets! Hannelore will not even pee in an outhouse, forget peeing in buckets.

Frau Schnadelhuber peers through her bifocals at Cleopatra

Maria's fastidious pencil markings, the multicoloured veins all over the map indicating twisting roads and rivers.

This country is too big to drive across, says Frau Schnadelhuber.

These motel beds are terrible, says Clotilde.

You could always do it on the floor, says Cleopatra Maria.

Hannelore makes coffee in the machine in the rented room.

This coffee is not bad, says Hannelore. But also not very good.

———

In Portage la Prairie, Hannelore scrubs and rinses out their stale, sweaty clothing with hot water and laundry detergent in the bathtub. She pokes once at the rinsed clothing swirling in the hot, steaming water, then leaves the bathroom to find more clothes. Clotilde surveys the collection of newspapers from all the gas stations they've visited.

These clothes in the bathtub just need to be wrung and dry, announces Hannelore, hands on her hips. Cleopatra Maria, come and help your Oma.

Ugh, says Cleopatra Maria, and she pouts her way to the bathroom and the clothes in the tub.

Do you have any more clothes you need washed? says Hannelore to Clotilde.

Oma! shouts Cleopatra from the bathroom.

Just wring and hang Cleopatra Maria, says Hannelore. Wring and hang. Easy.

But Oma!

What? Hannelore stamps her feet to the bathroom, her granddaughter lazy lazy lazy.

Hannelore almost screams at the black mess in the bathtub, the tub filled to the rim with runny, stinking mud.

Cleopatra Maria! says Hannelore. This is not funny. Not funny at all!

I didn't do it! I didn't do it!

Mud, says Clotilde from the doorway. All those clean clothes. Is that seaweed hanging from the shower-rod? No, I think it's your favourite white blouse Hannelore. Oh yes, and a little bit of seaweed.

Hannelore screams.

Time to go home, says Cleopatra Maria. Someone wants us to go home.

———

In Kenora, Ontario, they drink too much to celebrate the fact that they have finally reached Ontario, the province that holds Niagara Falls. Their clothes are permanently grey from the mud, but at least they are in Ontario.

Do you believe in ghosts? Cleopatra Maria asks Frau Schnadelhuber. Because I don't. But I don't understand that mud in the bathtub. There is no scientific explanation and I can't find anything on the Internet about it.

Of course there are ghosts, says Frau Schnadelhuber. But at some point ghosts are going to have to face the fact that they're dead and that's that. That person who did the mud, now he needs to see a good therapist and get on with being dead. And get away from that crummy motel. Living there forever would make anyone depressed.

But maybe we should go home, Frau Schnadelhuber. Maybe it's dangerous, says Cleopatra Maria.

It would take a lot more than a little mud to upset me, says Frau Schnadelhuber. Why, during the war sometimes all we had to eat was mud. I was happy if I could find a little bowl of mud for breakfast. Isn't that right, Clotilde?

Mud! says Clotilde. You were lucky to have mud for breakfast, Friedl. All we had to chew on was stones!

You lie, says Cleopatra Maria.

You respect your elders, says Frau Schnadelhuber. End of the history lesson.

In Kenora, one of the big tourist attractions is a giant fish on a pedestal. From the station wagon window, Hannelore looks at the giant fish, tries to put herself into the fish mind-set. Swimming under water, at home in the water. When they find a motel, Hannelore can't sleep she is so excited. She takes her brand new bicycle helmet, bought especially for the trip over the Falls, from her suitcase and straps it onto her head. She goes to the truck with her usher's flashlight, opens the sliding door in the cab and looks at the Niagara Ball. She opens the trap door. Straps herself inside. She is a giant fish.

In Thunder Bay, in the motel restaurant while picking the bacon out of her eight millionth Trans-Canada club sandwich, Cleopatra Maria knows she is being watched. She can feel eyes burrowing into the back of her head, they burrow so hard it hurts her and she knows that someone is trying to read her brain. She swivels her eyes from her plate to the source, her mouth still full of chicken, lettuce and brown toast, and sees a pimply teenage boy at another table, grinding into her with his eyes. Staring and staring and staring.

That boy is giving you the sex-eyes, whispers Frau Schnadelhuber into Cleopatra Maria's ear.

Cleopatra Maria looks at the boy. Her mouth makes a single chew, a cow in midthought.

I'm not *that* desperate, she says, and turns back to her plate. She hears the clink of her imaginary armour as she puts another slice of bacon on the side of her plate. She doesn't need sex anymore, she is the greatest, meanest, smartest virgin ever. Niven, and all of his kind, are ancient history.

New York, New York: Monday, October 21, 1996: 4:45 P.M.

Hamish travels with his show, his heart happy that he is a bachelor again, but he has a sad pain under his kilt. No cigar will make up for losing his Niagara Ball, it's been with him for years, his mascot, the little brother he never had, his own portable seduction hut. He saw Hannelore and those other nuts in the parking lot when they stole the Ball from the tunnels—he was stunned about how lack-adaisical they were about the whole thing, behaving like the Niagara Ball belonged to them, as though rolling it through the parking lot was the most natural thing to do. Watching them, he almost believed that the Ball did belong to them. He wanted to chase after them, get it back, but he knew that Hannelore was going to use it for what it was intended, he also knew that he would get into deep shit from the show's producers for using up good truck space for a huge ball made of pilfered materials from the show. So he hung up the phone after dialling 911.

False alarm, he said to the 911 operator sadly, and scratched under his baseball cap.

He should be happy that his baby is finally being used. He cries for three seconds, sharp and short like a typical macho bawl, then climbs farther up the ladder to the ceiling and the lights.

Ontario, Canada: October 23, 1996

St. Catharines, announces Cleopatra Maria. She reads the green sign aloud. We're almost at the Falls, Oma. Only fifteen more minutes and we're there I estimate.

Cleopatra Maria's hair frizzes around her head like a halo, she forgot to bring her curlers and hair dryer, lost her barrette in the last hotel room. Her hair is free as a bird and so is she.

We're almost there? says Hannelore. We're almost there, she repeats and her stomach jumps. She wears the blouse she wore when they began the journey over a week ago because she wants to look her best for when they arrive. Smells good as new.

———

St. Catharines, announces Frau Schnadelhuber. The day of reckoning has come.

Why do you always have to be so dramatic? grouches Clotilde. It bugs me when you play so dramatic.

Constipated from sitting so much, eh? Don't blame your plugups on me, I offered you the laxative tea.

I am tired of sitting in cars, I need to walk. I need to walk! Where is my cane, I am getting out to walk. Stop the truck, Clotilde says imperiously. I need my exercise!

Frau Schnadelhuber leans on the horn to announce they are stopping.

———

Uuugh! says Cleopatra Maria. Not agaaain! We're only fifteen minutes away!

Argh! says Hannelore. Not agaaain! Clotilde's constipated. She always gets like this when she's constipated. I told her to have some tea. She should have brought more bitters with her. I don't know why she only brought one bottle of Jägermeister.

That was good tea, says Cleopatra Maria. I feel clean as a whistle.

———

I'm not going on, says Clotilde. Leave and go without me. I refuse to sit in another vehicle. My bottom feels like it's been jammed up into my skull, my knees are stiff like broomsticks, my vertebrae have all fused together.

Clotilde hobbles around in a circle, leaning on her stick.

Look! she says. I've almost forgotten how to walk!

Frau Schnadelhuber pulls out her breasts.

Get in the truck, says Frau Schnadelhuber.

Okay, says Clotilde.

Cleopatra Maria helps Clotilde back into the cab of the truck. Hands Clotilde's cane up after her.

They drive on.

Niagara Falls, Canada: Wednesday, October 23, 1996

And when Cleopatra Maria sees the Falls she thinks, *Yeah right.*

The falls are enormous, the rush of the water pouring over the rocks, not water but a beast. The town of Niagara Falls a solid mass of tourist trap hotels, freakish overpriced museums, and neon. Cleopatra Maria hates it all at first sight.

When Frau Schnadelhuber sees the Falls she thinks, *What am I doing here?*

In the tunnels under the river, like German tourists and not the law-breakers they are about to become, they wear their yellow plastic rain ponchos and Frau Schnadelhuber from under her hood stares at the water falling in front of them that doesn't look a thing like water. There is no way to understand it as water, the grey light, the swirling clouds of mist. Not water because water as Frau Schnadelhuber understands it is controlled and separate, in sinks and in pools. In tubs and buckets. Water is to be dominated and used. Water shouldn't have impulses of its own. This water, the most natural water she has ever seen, is the most unnatural water she has ever seen.

In their outfits of thin yellow plastic, the water so loud they have to yell to hear each other and can't even hear each other then, Hannelore certainly can't hear anything anyone says while they are in the tunnels. The "Danger" signs in red and black and white, pictures of people crawling over the rails. They are going to crawl over the rails.

Hannelore smiles so hard she wants to scream because at last she is *home*.

Yeah right, thinks Cleopatra Maria and, without realizing it, she sticks her thumb in her mouth.

I need to smoke, says Frau Schnadelhuber. Let's find a bar and smoke. Is there any place around here where there's a bar where I could smoke?

Her hands tremble as they dig through her purse for the cigarette. She needs to smoke that badly.

Cleopatra Maria drives the station wagon, her Oma in the passenger's seat, Tante Clotilde and Frau Schnadelhuber in the back, and they drive around and around the town of Niagara Falls, down the streets filled with neon signs and wax museums, house-sized haunted castles.

This place is a shit-hole, says Cleopatra Maria. This place offends me. I want to go home.

There, says Frau Schnadelhuber. There, the Capri. That looks like my kind of place.

They sit in the Capri at tables covered in stained orange terrycloth, their waitress a grumpy, older woman.

We've driven here all the way from the other side of the country, chirps Cleopatra Maria.

Izzat so, says the waitress.

You're bitter, says Cleopatra Maria recognizing a kindred spirit. How long you been working here?

Since 1901, says the waitress. She slams a bottle of beer down onto the table.

Couldn't find no other job, she says. Tried to sell postcards but you can't live offa *postcards.*

Your dress looks like 1901, says Frau Schnadelhuber, suddenly gay with her cigarettes and glasses of alcohol surrounding her.

Can I see some I.D., says the waitress to Cleopatra Maria.

I'm twenty-six!

Get outta the bar. Get outta this town.

What?

Get outta the bar, you're a minor. Alla you, *get outta my bar! Get outta this town!*

We're finishing our drinks, says Clotilde.

No, says the waitress and suddenly she turns her eyes full on Cleopatra Maria and shouts with a voice that sounds like she is yelling under water: *Fucking tourists stay away from my river.*

Too bad, says Frau Schnadelhuber on the street in front of the Capri. That was a very good bar.

Cleopatra Maria remembers the watery grey of the waitress's eyes and suddenly she understands too much. The eyes had no pupils. They were the colour of drowning.

Do you know who that was, Oma? says Cleopatra Maria, her face suddenly sweaty from the heat of revelation, the muscles in her stomach clenched into many fists. Do you know who that was?

Who? says Hannelore. But Hannelore cares more about getting her cholesterol pills out of the leather pouch around her neck.

That was her, says Cleopatra Maria. That was *her*. *She* put the mud in the bathtub to warn us away. She hoped I would drive drunk. She doesn't want us to do this. She doesn't want you to go over the Falls.

Cleopatra Maria's teeth begin to chatter, her body suddenly aching from the hypothermia Annie's body has been enduring for ninety-five years.

The last thing the waitress said before she kicked them out: *It's mine. I am the first and the last.*

In the morning just as the sun gets up, they drive to the Falls with the Niagara Ball. Cleopatra Maria pulls out the champagne that's been rolling around in the station wagon all this time, she drinks none of it—since four nights ago she can't stand the smell or look of champagne anymore. Since last night, she's realized who sold the champagne to her. The champagne mostly froths onto the ground, but she manages to pour some into the cups they use to brush their teeth.

No one notices the three old women and the homely girl with the oversized head on the shore of the river near the truck. They are as invisible as the ushers and ticket-takers in the largest auditorium west of Manitoba.

They toast. Prosit, they say and Hannelore cries and Cleopatra Maria cries and Frau Schnadelhuber cries. Cleopatra Maria helps the women into the Niagara Ball one by one.

You probably don't need your cane Tante Clotilde, she says to Clotilde. I love you Oma. I love you Tante, I love you Frau Schnadelhuber.

Cleopatra Maria slides closed the trap door. Hannelore bolts it from the inside.

Hannelore smiles so hard she cannot speak. She flicks on the light in the dark. The tiny bulb flickers, then burns out. Goddamn Hamish.

Hannelore left her hearing aid in her suitcase.

Friendly tourists in American flag leather jackets see Cleopatra Maria struggling to roll the giant egg full of women and help her roll the Ball over the wrought-iron bannister. The Niagara Ball bobs in the river and begins the jagged, lurching journey to the precipice. Cleopatra Maria sits herself high up in the driver's seat of the one-ton. She will drive to the bottom to greet them when they get out. She has always wanted to drive a one-ton. At the bottom, she will call an ambulance, but not the police.

The Falls refuse to be merely a symbol. The Falls keep falling because they couldn't care less; whoever chooses to jump in them, cry in them, die in them doesn't matter one bit. The water licks over the rim of the cliffs, a violent ending, the smooth skin of the water, smooth as a Sunday morning swim.

The Niagara Ball full of women goes up and over and down the chutes and the Falls couldn't care less.

The tourists on shore shout when the bright ball bursts from the water, brighter than the sun, hotter and more dangerous. The paramedics paste the brown paper bag over Cleopatra Maria's nose and mouth.

Showers of water, bouncing balls, the air crisp and October delicious. The low season. Janitor Alvarez continues his cleaning rounds in the tunnels.

The bright flashing lights of the police cruisers and ambulance give their flamboyant Good Morning, their lights reflected on the slick, wet sides of the vessel.

Such a beautiful country, such outrageously sparkling water.

When other daredevils tempted the Falls or the rapids, her feat was recalled as ancient history, but no one checked to see if she was still alive. Only when she entered the county infirmary (the poorhouse) was there a brief flurry. Annie resisted this ignominy to the last. "I've done what no other woman in the world had nerve to do," she told Louis Elmer, commissioner of charities, "only to become a pauper."

—Pierre Berton, Niagara: A History of the Falls

Here are the deaths:

Hannelore's dental plate. Broken in half, the impact of her jaws crashing into one another when the Niagara Ball hit bottom. At the hotel "Nous parlons français & wir sprechen Deutsch," she asks for porridge and coffee. Has to pass on the slightly chewy white bread with plum compote. The inside of her left cheek bleeds a little at the hotel so she doesn't drink very much of the hot coffee.

Frau Schnadelhuber's Dirndl Kleid. The skirt ripped off completely. The three women don't know exactly how, but most of the skirt is in Clotilde's hands when they come to. The bodice ripped and one of her breasts naked and flopping like a fleshy string-bean into the world. The police and paramedics help Frau Schnadelhuber to shore and at first she can barely hobble from the shock, the incredible cold sweeping over her body, the flashes of camera bulbs and whirring lights from the police cruisers. But she looks down and sees her single naked breast, her naked legs, her underpants and her support-hose showing, and suddenly she feels like she should break into the Can-Can like she's at the Folies Bergere. She does begin to break into the Can-Can, low kicks but still the Can-Can—she feels that high in the sky—but then two policemen grab each of her arms and escort her to a squad car.

Also her dental plate. Cracked from the high pitch of her scream when Janitor Alvarez kicked them out of the tunnel entrance. She asks for oatmeal and an ashtray and coffee. Also a ripe banana she can mash and spoon into her mouth. She bit her tongue, not hard, but hard enough to cut it, so she waits for her coffee to almost go cold before she drinks.

Clotilde's hearing aid. She shouldn't have worn it, Hannelore told her it was stupid to wear it, Clotilde played dumb, she didn't want to miss hearing the roar of the water when they were actually in it. Come all this way and not even get to hear what's going on? Come on!

Hannelore couldn't hear a goddamn thing, thinks Clotilde, missed the whole trip and made conversations up in her head and talked to them.

Also Clotilde's dental plate. Her jaws cracked the plate into pieces from anxiety and excitement and she almost choked on a fragment. At the hotel she eats stewed prunes. She eats them and they are the best goddamn thing she has tasted in years, today, the day of her death. She could do a million jumping-jacks she feels so alive. Later, she will nap for almost twenty-four hours.

Karl. Tries his own barrel when he hears about his ex-wife Friedl, sees her picture in the paper. Niagara River is not so kind with Karl and turns him and his badly built barrel into Karl-porridge at the foot of the falls. Karl-minestrone by the time he and the barrel have reached the suck of the whirlpool. His entrails make the seagulls vomit. Rotten through and through. Bastard.

Hannelore's hair. The paramedics and police, so eager to get them out of the vessel, dunk the women in the water and Hannelore's hair flattens out, of course her hair was ruined from the sweat pouring down her skull, the bicycle helmet flattening out the curls (of course she had her hair done before the expedition got under way), but still she had it better under control before the police got their hands on it. She is furious. She can see her bright pink scalp through the white soggy strands of hair. She wears her beige headscarf at the breakfast table. Tucks her hairs underneath, first thing after breakfast she will have to get her hair done. As soon as they pay the fine. As soon as Dieter delivers the bail money.

Really, they shouldn't have been allowed a second breakfast, but old people need to eat or they get disoriented, and Hannelore whined her special whine, the whine that bores into skulls and eats away at tender brain flesh. The porridge is fine. Her teeth are missing. The grate of the dull edge of the spoon on her gums. She feels one of her bottom teeth loosen.

Hannelore. After Dieter gets his hands on her in a giant hug of desperation, irritation, and alarm, after he has to pay the bail, breaks a dozen Canada Savings Bonds to do it, Yes Mutti, the ones I was saving to send Cleopatra Maria to Latin camp in Saskatchewan next summer.

Rosario asks Hannelore to pose for a Niagara Falls sculpture made entirely of faux fur.

Also dead. One of Janitor Alvarez's shoes from last week. One hundred and twelve used condoms. A charm bracelet. Six tennis balls. Two bras. One ring finger. A priceless clip-on earring. Twelve engagement rings: seven zirconia, four diamond, one plastic. Three virginities. Microscopic fragments from the super-rubber surface of Hamish's Niagara Ball.

The empty bottle of champagne. Cleopatra Maria realizes that throwing the emptied bottle in the River is the same thing as pollution, but she wants to christen the vessel, even if only in a symbolic way. The bottle snags on the bottom of the river bed before it can even reach the edge of the precipice and the water whips the label off and onward.

Here are the deaths:

Frau Hannelore Schmitt, Fräulein Clotilde Starfinger, Frau Friedl Schnadelhuber pounded to bits by water on the rocks of Niagara Falls.

I'm telling you, says Clotilde, The only way to describe it is that one minute I was dead, the next minute I was alive. That is all I have to say. Not a thing like butter in a churn!

Mrs. Anna Edson Taylor of old age and poverty. Her sixty-three-year-old body survived the pounding water of the Falls and she was christened "Queen of the Mist," but it was the world outside the river that finally murdered her and she died at the age of eighty-three, destitute and alone. Obscurity consumed her and spit her out in pieces.

While Hannelore, Clotilde and Friedl gum their porridge and mashed fruit, in her grave Annie's bones stop their comfortable shift to the North and begin to seethe. The bones grind the cemetery soil in fury, the blades in a food processor, she has been cheated yet again, she was the first and the last the first and the last the first and thelastthefirstandthelast.

Annie was the first, the oldest, the bravest, the best. And for almost a hundred years other showy, upstart, screw-loose daredevils have tried to take her title away from her with their fancy expensive barrels and machines. Upstarts, thrill-seekers, young men with time, old men with money. Those daredevils do it for thrills and so they can brag at dinner parties. She did it because she had no choice. She is being perpetually eclipsed. Cheated.

Cleopatra Maria hears the bright sizzle of Annie's bones over the chewing and mumbling and can no longer eat because of the racket of Annie's ghost.

Have another French toast, mumbles Hannelore to Cleopatra Maria. Another French toast will put flesh on your bones.

And hair on your chest, mumbles Friedl. Hey Clotilde, Cleopatra Maria's not listening. Losing her hearing and only in her twenties.

Then Friedl remembers that Clotilde lost her hearing-aid in the Niagara Ball.

Cleopatra Maria prepares herself to meet with Annie. Finally have constructive dialogue instead of scary, crabby waitresses; bathtubs full of mud. Cleopatra Maria is no therapist, but she prepares herself as best she can anyway to deal with a depressed and furious 158-year-old woman. She puts on her born-again virgin's armour, designed it herself, and glides from her body in the hotel restaurant to Annie's furious bones across the Canadian-American border.

Hey! says Friedl, Hey! and she shakes Cleopatra Maria's shoulder. Come back here and finish your breakfast!

Cleopatra Maria lands in the cemetery right in the middle of Annie's racket. Cleopatra Maria stands for a moment watching the bubbling earth and when the bones crown and the cemetery earth crumbles upward, Cleopatra Maria steps forward.

Excuse me! Cleopatra Maria calls.

The bones stop their furious grind upward through the dirt. Propped in the earth, they listen for one second.

I know who you are, says Cleopatra Maria.

The bones resume their pushing until they are free of the earth and then whip into the air and begin to smash at the air and whatever object stands in the way.

They pull up tree roots, crack tombstones, pound earthworms into fleshy little puddings.

Hey! shouts Cleopatra Maria. I'm trying to talk to you! I think a dialogue would be beneficial for both of us!

A femur whizzes at Cleopatra Maria's head, she ducks, and the bone thunks into the ground. Cleopatra Maria throws her body on to the femur to stop it from braining her. The other femur whizzes up behind her and starts to beat Cleopatra Maria on the back of the legs.

Are you with the ghost? says Friedl, Cleopatra Maria answer me!

Cleopatra Maria nods. Hannelore and Clotilde continue chewing in their naked hearing-aid silence.

Is it that woman? says Friedl. Annie?

Cleopatra Maria nods.

While Cleopatra Maria wrestles the femurs, Annie's floating ribs try to stab her in the back, knuckle bones aim for her eyes. Annie's bones pound at the metal covering Cleopatra Maria's body and

Cleopatra Maria covers her head with her arms, hears a thousand tin cans.

Annie, gasps Cleopatra Maria, what's your problem? You will always be the first. Not the oldest, not the last, but always the first. The best. The bravest.

The furious knock knock knock of a finger bone on Cleopatra Maria's helmet.

Mrs. Taylor! she shouts. Listen to me!

A scapula frisbees into Cleopatra Maria's back, ricochets straight up into the air, and lands a centimetre away from Cleopatra Maria's painfully naked Adam's apple.

You tell her to come have some breakfast, says Friedl, Tell her there's plenty. I'll have the waitress set another place at the table!

Friedl scans the room for the waitress who's in the back of the kitchen, kissing the cook. Friedl stands up, still a little sore from the trip, and hobbles to the restaurant work-station. She gets out a fork, knife, spoon, bowl and plate. Also a coffee cup. She pours coffee into the cup and sets everything on a tray.

Tell her to come eat! shouts Friedl at Cleopatra Maria. Eating with friends is good for the soul!

We would like you to join us for breakfast, Cleopatra Maria slowly tells the scapula. The coffee is very good my Oma says.

The scapula flips away. Flips again. All of Annie starts to flip, a fish tossed on land.

Friedl sets the extra place setting, pulls a chair from another table.

There, she says.

Cleopatra Maria waits to make sure the bones aren't trying to trick her. She slowly reaches out and catches a bone, strokes calm the flipping bone with the pad of her thumb, then catches another bone with her other hand. She sits up and reaches to the bones littered and flipping around her. Strokes them one by one. Cleopatra Maria pats the skull like a dog when it finally stops rolling, bends her head to listen to the pelvis just in case.

Cleopatra Maria lies down next to the bones.

You saved their lives, she whispers.

The bones completely still.

Friedl watches the woman gather her skirts around her, the skirts dripping large blobs of mud, dead fish, and Niagara River garbage. The woman seats herself at the extra place setting at the table, Hannelore and Clotilde too busy eating to notice.

Friedl smiles broadly. Blinks only once at the smell.

Come, says Friedl. Eat.

Phoo, mumbles Clotilde to her plate. Friedl, you farted.

That's better, nicht? says Friedl to the woman. Everything in order. Try some of the coffee. Surprisingly good, we think.

Friedl pushes the filled cup of coffee across the table.

Cleopatra Maria pulls a handkerchief, more environmental than Kleenex, from her sleeve and offers it to Annie's pocked and bloated, but well-dressed, remains. So Annie can wipe away the tears and get on with her breakfast.

Hannelore, Clotilde, and Friedl can buy the delicatessen because they do what Annie Taylor in 1901 refused to do.

I am forty-two years old, said Annie Taylor. Not a minute older.

Later she would have a falling out with her brother, Montgomery, that lasted until her death because he wanted to tell the world that she was actually sixty-three. Not a minute younger.

Forty-two, she repeated.

North America enjoyed her for a little while, then forgot. To make money, she posed for tourists with a replica of her barrel—the original barrel stolen from her by her manager almost immediately after the great stunt—and tried to sell postcards of herself on streetcorners. Later she offered her services as a clairvoyant, but she never made much money. She said she would go over the Falls again but never did. Finally she died. She sold too few postcards of herself on too many corners beside a replica of the barrel that almost became her coffin.

I am seventy-five years old, says Hannelore. My name is Mrs. Heinrich Schmitt, and I need to phone my son and daughter-in-law. Hannelore's hair in straggles, her hands shaking, mouth bleeding.

I am eighty-five, says Clotilde. She pulls the blanket tightly around her and her gums begin to mutter.

I will be one hundred and twenty-four next September, sings Frau Schnadelhuber and she claps her hands in the air and begins to dance. I smoke a pack a day and look at me!

They make exactly twenty thousand dollars from the book deal and Frau Schnadelhuber agrees to pose topless for a Toronto art magazine and a San Francisco lesbian nudie magazine. The city's right-wing magazine reprints the photo with a black band across

Frau Schnadelhuber's exposed breasts and calls her a "nympho granny." Hedwig buys twenty copies of the magazine and hands them out to her friends. Her mother the daredevil.

Frau Schnadelhuber's breasts, still glistening with Niagara River water, will be remembered forever.

Edmonton, Canada. 1996

Clotilde holds a fax from the Madame in her hands. She puts it down on the delicatessen counter.

This Madame, says Clotilde. Is she crazy or just brainless?

No, says Oma Hupfel. Just bored and old. She has no family. She says she is tired of having so many things. She wants her things to be well taken care of when she's gone.

But the Niagara Ball? The fax says she will trade the deli for the Niagara Ball.

What am I going to do? says Oma Hupfel. Can I stay here, Frau Schnadelhuber?

You're a lazy worker, says Frau Schnadelhuber. Admit it.

Yes, I am a lazy worker.

I don't steal things. Admit it.

You don't steal things, you haven't stolen a thing in your life. I have stolen everything.

All right, you can stay.

Hannelore daydreams about the delicious food they will cook. Ida will come work for them. Not as a waitress, Ida would make a terrible waitress. Maybe as a hostess. Hannelore will make Cleopatra Maria eat at least three square meals every day.

The Englishman John Maude tells of a New York lawyer who arrived in 1800, took one look, said, "Is that all?" and journeyed on without even bothering to get off his horse.

—DONALDSON, GORDON. Niagara! The Eternal Circus.

The shopping mall is fine, the delicatessen is fine, everything is fine, everything is too fine.

I need a window in here, says Clotilde. I am suffocating without a window.

This is a shopping mall, says Frau Schnadelhuber, there are no such things as windows in shopping malls.

Frau Schnadelhuber wears a purple push-up bra and jeans. And a butcher's apron.

Clotilde hobbles on her cane to the art store on the other side of the shopping mall and buys a canvas and acrylic paints.

She calls Rosario. Give me some lessons, Clotilde says.

Rosario tries to teach Clotilde the fundamentals of landscape painting: No, no, says Rosario, Look, your trees are bigger than your mountains!

But Clotilde paints landscapes anyway, German fields full of yellow flowers and the Rocky Mountains in the distance. A few paintings have tiny Sasquatches in them hidden in the trees. She hangs her landscapes all over the delicatessen. They are terrible, but mostly the women who come to eat don't care. They drink their decaffeinated coffee (better for blood pressure says Ida), or sip laxative tea (delicious! says Dot) and look out the false windows at the gooey trees and lumpy clouds. Very good food, the customers say. And very comfortable.

The women who come there, come to put their feet up, to escape their families, or to find company and be visible in a group of very present women. The food is cheap and German and fills the stomach, doggie bags are mandatory even if there is no food left over. Frau Schnadelhuber, Clotilde and Hannelore rename the delicatessen "Königin der Nebel," Queen of the Mist.

It's a dumb name, says Cleopatra Maria. Sounds like a massage parlour. Or a steam bath.

Eat your red cabbage, says Hannelore.

Eat it yourself! retorts Cleopatra Maria. She fiddles with a bone strung on a chain around her neck. A human knuckle bone, but no one has to know that.

Hannelore and Cleopatra Maria stare blankly at each other. Hannelore realizes she will need to find some sex, crashing, over-whelming Niagara Falls kind of sex, but soon.

Cleopatra Maria has made a date to see Niven tomorrow. She will invite him to the delicatessen to meet the women and then she will seduce him in the back room—her own daredevil stunt she's decided. Friedl has shown Cleopatra Maria some premature ejacu-lation prevention tricks with the help of a carrot. Cleopatra Maria, Hannelore, Clotilde and Friedl will celebrate Cleopatra Maria's burst hymen with a great big apple Strudel and plenty of music.

The sasquatches in their trees, the queen in her mist, and Cleopatra Maria's discarded virginity will all nod and clap along to the oom-pa-pa beat.